Canticle Mythos Series

Anthology I:

THE FIRST SIRES

Limited Revised Edition.

Cover Art by Caelan Stokkermans / Illustrations by Abril Martinez
Logos, Maps by Maxwell Aston / Written by Matthew R.R. Morrese
Edited by Corwin Zahn / Published by Canticles Productions LLC
ISBN: 978-0-692-16867-7
12039 Avery Lane
Bridgeton, Missouri 63304

Accounts Recollected

by

Mimyr, the Second

Histories Penned

by

Matthew R.R. Morrese

Histories Edited

by

Corwin Zahn

Illustrations Brought to Life

by

Abril Martinez

For the current Canticles Productions Family:
(as of August, 2018)
Alexander James Adams / Sarah Ambrosio
Aubree Bowen / Ruslan Batenko / Jaidyn Carroll
Matthew Gardner / Sandra Greenberg / Abril Martinez
Cathy McManamon / Matthew R.R. Morrese
Krishel Alise Penrose / Caelan Stokkermans
Brittany Torres / Corwin Zahn

&

A special thanks to our **Patreon Members:**
(as of August, 2018)
Paige Accalia / K Van Brunt / Noel & Talya Carroll
Eva Davis / Justin Delgado / Jan DiMasi
Dain / Xap Esler / Debbie Fligor / Samuel Greenberg
The Nicest Man on Earth / Lisa Hawkridge
Julie Howard / Robert Klobe / Sharon Laubach
Stephanie Leiva / Anna Miller / Luke Miller
Sam Mullin / Ron Oakes / Pierre E. Pettinger, Jr.
Eric Ray / Debora Reinert / Jennifer Rocca
Sylvia Salas / Kathy Schopp / Cynthia Sloniker
Nioclas Smith / Kei Striker / Lori Vickers
Catherine Weaver / Heather West / Heather York

The Limited Revised Edition is dedicated to all those
who prefer turning an aged page, rather than swiping
left on a silly screen, to all those who prefer driving to
flying, and to all those who prefer adventure and
romantics over apathy and rumination.
-MRRM

CONTENTS.

The First Sires

An Orsain's Account 01

A Bayman's Burden 37

An Elvar's Edict 63

A Reignman's River 93

An Eleaos'i's Abandon 111

A Nûmunyr's Crusade 141

An Evendain's Exchange 185

A Clansman's Folly 197

The Myrmen's Might 213

A Wreathelander's Wrath 227

A Fyrzhor's Fall 251

The Nameless 275

Concerning Mythology: In any mythology, we tend to focus on gods; in our case, the Eldûn – the Astar, the Ildraeor, and the Elzhri. Doing so lacks the proper time considered and thought given to that of "mortal man". The undying outshine the dying. Or, we focus on heroes and villains, an army instead of a soldier, the flock instead of a single sheep, the nameless that have been forgotten to time.

There were twelve races Aegis bore us, defined by their look, culture, religion, or civilized Realm, who appeared and evolved during the Age of Origin. Origin is defined as the first thousand years of Aegis' history – when the Ildraeor fashioned the scape of Her body, the Astar forged Her whispers into language, and the Elzhri, as nature-manifest, walked the world among mortals. The twelve races were nurtured by Aegis, and guided by these Eldûn, until Chaos bathed Her in bedlam's fire at Age's End.

Therefore, we take a step back from the names and numbers the Athenaeum's chroniclers collect, recount, and emphasize to look at those who played a role as individuals of lost memory, the little things and greater kinships that might have been lost if not for these tales. It was these peoples and races that gave Aegis Her meaning and purpose during the Age of Origin, because lives are so much more valuable if finite.

All tales are recounted here as best as we could avail them, as Mimyr herself sits afore me to help my hand along where I may forget. Consider this a reflection of our peoples. These are the First Sires.

E.

An Orsain's Account

Iödas, first of Orphaeon & Nûmyri, first of the Freemares

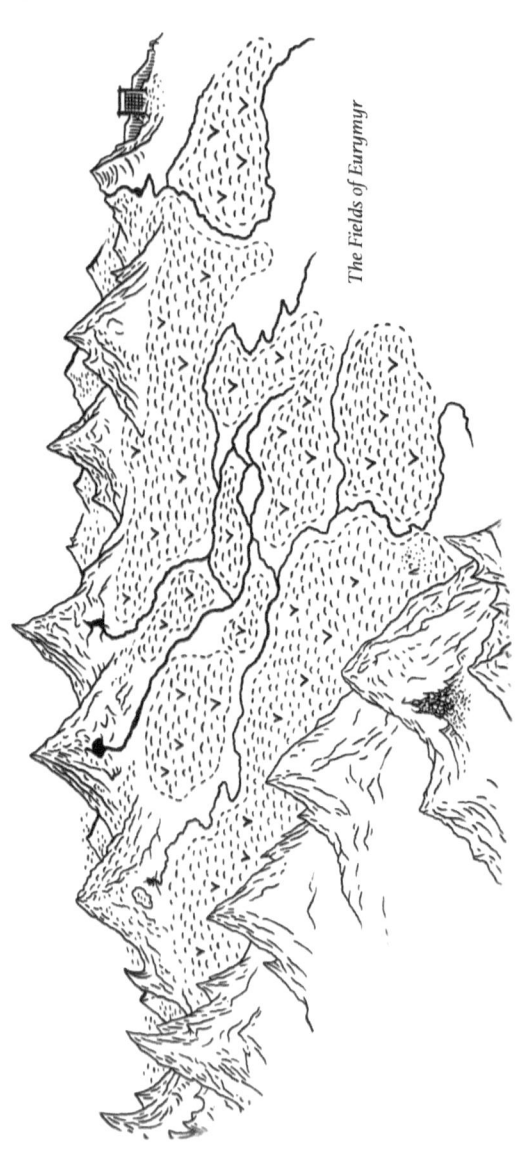

The Fields of Eurymyr

...being a short story during the Age of Origin,
approximately in the year 629...

Iödas watched them drag his master away.

Just moments before, the Orsain Horselord shined magnificent, all glory and might, in kingly exaltation to the crowd's applause. Iödas had burnished the lord's steel – armor, flanks, and spurs – by the light of constellations recounting legends even greater than his master's, as if encouraging the son-squire's hand, promising that of victory on the morrow. He'd taken the road to the temple of Dûnkrath atop Mount Dûn-evare at dawn's peak to offer one of their best mares to the almighty Wrathlord, a sacrifice to incur the god's blessing through blood, prayed in the hopes to retain the champion's seat on the tourney grounds for a sixth consecutive year.

Presently, Iödas observed in great expectation as the adversaries spurred their steeds forward.

When the son-squire saw the lance-point strike the Eorlin's neck, gorge through the other end and bloody the jousting arm down to the stock, his heart dropped in a falling beat of despair – he knew immediately, it was all over for his master ... and him. His knees hit the soil and sunk deep into the mud torn up by a hundred hooves in their clopping to-and-fros across the fairegrounds that week. All true-bled Orsain were masters and tamers of the faithful beasts, but it was the nobles of the aristocracy born into their rightful place as Oisin's Horselords that ruled the Thoroughfaire. They were all men of profound stature, beauty and strength, with hair of yellow and eyes frighteningly fierce.

Iödas watched them drag his master, no longer beautiful; his lord, no longer profound; his father, no longer breathing, away.

As for his own eyes, the squire's were unlike an Orsain's – dark; they were as dark as his hair before his father dyed it yellow to match his sire. The old Eorlin said blood was thicker than faith, less volatile in nature, and his faith had surely failed him today. *Dûnkrath be damned*, he thought.

Iödas knew Orsain bastards were castigated from Oisin at birth, that's just the way it was – they were seen as a slight on purity; however, to worsen his lineage, Iödas' mother wasn't even Oisin-born. Only in the secret Shadows of the night did his father recount memories of his mother, but how romantic they were: She was a beauty beyond kinship, beyond belief and from the Northlands, across the Fields of Eurymyr, which itself was named after a fallen star who embodied a mortal woman, a commoner given the power to hear the whispers of Aegis. Alas, that was a fairy tale. Regrettably, his mother was no star. Nor was she Orsain. Accounting for the last minute of his father's glorious life, Iödas was now a bastard and orphan both.

The cheers of the crowd echoed in his throbbing ears as if applauding the grim future the fatestreams cut in front of him; it resonated off the shock refusing to subside. There was a tapping on his shoulder; when he didn't answer, a gloved hand forcefully spun him on his knees, pulling him from his paralysis, and meeting him with a cold, hard stare. It was a woman with locks the color of the sun braided beneath her coif and mail fashioned to fit her curves. Her cloudy eyes pierced his recent longing. His own mother would've looked nothing like this. She was no warrior, but a maiden of the mountains.

In contrast, pure-bled Oisin women, so long as their virtue was intact, rode bareback, shot arrow and threw javelin while mounted, and fought as formidably as any male counterpart. They did not lay aside their virginity until they'd killed a man in battle, and they did not wed until they were prepared to trade the soldier's mantle with that of motherhood. A woman who took a husband laid down her reins willingly, no longer bled for anyone but her children unless compelled by war.

Iödas gave no resistance when she led him away; he merely stared back at the grounds in waning terror. The tournament concluded, its prize won, during his moments of grief, and the crowd of commoners fed back into the daily life of Oisin's elitist society.

That night Iödas slept in the *orkosdûn*, Oisin's single prison house, and his nightmares forced him to relive every moment – he watched them drag his master, lord, father away, over and over and over again.

A fortnight passed in the cold and dark of the *orkosdûn*, until his father no longer haunted his dreamsteps. This opened the gates for the whispers of Aegis, visions in warning and prophecy, to approach his mind. In his sleep, he began to wade through the fatestreams, and the rivers took hold of him in their currents, clutching tight and dragging him unto oracular dream.

Iödas' eyes were trained south where Oisin cavalry trotted a pace slow, in loose formation – a military wedge. *Was this a battle*, he thought, *where am I?* The cavalry closed as they approached the enemy – Iödas and those about him – and two hundred meters out let fly a volley of arrows. A boy next to Iödas was struck down, but another replaced him immediately; he stood in a defensive line of pikemen who stood unbelievably steadfast, controlling their overwhelming fear of death without thought or pause. Fifty meters out, the cavalry turned away, their mounts refusing to rush the unflinching barricade.

Their second charge found more success when another flurry of arrows struck true their mark, gutting a significant hole in the line just a few feet from Iödas; it was impossible to seal in the split seconds a battle allowed. The warhorses closed ranks on instinct and rushed the opportunity, breaking through the line in all grace and rage. One boy was hit at full gallop by an Oisin lance couched tight; the lancer held firm in his saddle, but the poor pikeman was heaved backward, thrown with such momentum his entire column fell in effect, two more wounded in the process.

The shield wall broken, the wedged cavalry blossomed out in a tight sunburst formation that scattered the defense. Unfortunately for the attackers, the boys that surrounded Iödas were not about to flee as an ordinary man would expect of another; instead, the children reengaged and closed in tight around the sunburst, taking the offensive two- and three-to-one at a time.

Amidst this new bedlam, Iödas saw the men on horseback were golden-haired and leathered, the very Oisin Horselords his father belonged to before his fall. In contrast, the boys all about him were everything but golden, black and brown and red-haired bastards all, but clad in steel, helm to toe. They were anywhere between seven and thirteen, but could not possibly be any older. It was a golden army versus a muddy throng.

A horseman next to Iödas drove forward, barreled past him and over two others – one small with greasy locks of dull flame, another muscular and bald. They rose in unison with barely a scratch to their plate.

Unfortunately, the rider found an opening between breast and pauldron of the little one, and his lance took advantage of it. It pierced the child, collar to spleen. However, by the time the boy dropped, his taller compatriot's longsword found its mark with a cry of vengeance, thrust easily through the horseman's leathered ribs. The rider's mount reared, throwing the lancer wildly away. He landed at Iödas' feet, eyes paling in death. The son-squire watched the blood pool around his boots, a crimson tide that melted away into a sea of liquid silver.

When Iödas looked up, he was no longer on the battlefield, but above it. He stood on the parapet of a stronghold. The rivers of silver sanguine ran along half-pipes draining into cauldrons set within the wall on spits. This guided his gaze down to a regiment of Oisin infantry hammering at the stronghold's gates with a golden, horse-headed ram.

He watched as a child-steward flurried past him and poured the contents of the cauldrons one by one over the encroachers. The sanguine darkened into crude oil on its way down, splattering over the foot soldiers. A lit match floated down thereafter and set them asunder.

The enemy were no doubt Orsain from Oisin itself; but, *who are these children?* Iödas thought. There was a deafening crash of stone into stone, and the parapet beneath Iödas collapsed. The ram was a diversion – there was alchemy here.

He landed hard on the impossible. It was the largest anvil he'd ever seen. Made of gold and garnet, it could only be the anvil of Dûnkrath himself. When Iödas stood atop it, he saw lesser anvils surrounding him of pitch black iron, ore pure and shining in the light shed from the golden altar. He felt pressure, then a puncture through the softer flesh at his temples. When his fingers made to run through his golden hair, a spear thrust through his clavicle – he cried out!

A black crown tumbled from his head and clattered to the floor, stained with the dye of his lie. He looked up at his enemy; he saw a raven-haired reflection of himself in his father's eyes. The old Eorlin cut through the silence with his thick, brusque declaration, "I am dead. You are no man's son, now."

Iödas woke, his ears ringing and head throbbing. He ran his fingers through his hair, found nothing but muss and mud caked into it, an effect of sleeping on the soiled floor of the *orkosdûn*. There was no crown; there was no anvil; there was no wound other than that his father left in siring him. A splash of frozen water tore him abruptly from reverie.

"I said, let's go!" an Oisin prison guard repeated. The cell was open, and the *ogri* of a man was waiting for him.

Iödas was thrown into the back of an open cart with five other prisoners. They were each fettered at the ankle, and the *orkosdûn* guard was quick to shackle Iödas and get back to work, surely unfavorable to whatever cellmates Iödas left behind in that wicked house.

Iödas was overcome when he saw his fellow passengers. He immediately recognized the red-haired boy sitting across from him, the boy from his dream, no older than seven. He rocked back and forth on the bench seat. There was a sadness when he spoke, "Is today that day, Haeseus?"

And the second was indeed the taller, balding figure in his vision, muscles tone and gleaning in the morning light, "Aye, Mouse. This fancy sealed our fate."

They were talking about him, Iödas saw it in their eyes, glaring at him and his golden hair. They shipped them off in sets of six, so his arrival marked their departure. The weeks spent in prison was simply a formality, in case there was a mistake. There was never a mistake. Now, he had no choice but to respond, or his forthcoming servitude could quickly turn dangerous. "Your fathers sentenced you here by laying out of wedlock, not I."

A third boy, sitting on the other side of Haeseus, jerked forward, stayed only by his manacles. A scar traced from a blind eye down to his jaw line, creasing grotesquely when he spat back, "If I wasn't chained, I'd ring your little neck, fancy. My father was a good man."

Iödas shrugged, unamused. He would not be threatened by the likes of these bullies, "Then blame yourself for not dying at birth. Regardless, we all break the law by existing."

Haeseus hadn't taken his eyes off the son-squire, "You're pretty sure of yourself for a bastard."

"You're pretty aggressive for a slave."

"How dare—!" the ugly one started until he was stopped by Haeseus, who obviously had some power over this company.

"This is Mud the Mad," he offered, "He's a little intemperate. His quieter kin there," Haeseus motioned to the scrawny, yet similarly structured boy that sat across from Mud, "is Thatch. They're both loose sons of the Thatched Council, Second Seat, who sent them away as soon as they were strong enough to stand on their own." He pointed to the youth sitting next to Iödas, whose eyes stared blankly across the Fields of Eurymyr, "We call him Mute. Cause he's mute. Or so we think. As far as we know, like little Mouse here, he was found on the streets, an orphan, most likely for illegitimacy of his birth, abandoned to the sewers and found by the city guard. Lastly, my dear Mouse here was feeding off mice when they found him."

Iödas nodded, "Mud, Thatch, Mouse, and Mute. Okay, so, who are you? By the looks of you, I'd call you *ogri*." Iödas wanted to know if Haeseus would take the bait. He'd heard the boy's name when Mouse addressed him earlier, but did Haeseus know this? And did he have a temper of his own?

He didn't; instead, he smiled and gave a slight, though well-conditioned, bow in their all-too-close quarters. It was an ambassadorial contrast to his barbaric figure, "I am Haeseus, of the Aerseusi. Stablesons. My father kept me as long as he could. When they finally came to take me away, he let them."

Iödas kept his eyes trained on the stableson. He knew what was coming.

At length, Haeseus obliged, "I wonder, now, who are you?"

Iödas didn't hesitate, "I am Iödas, son-squire to Eirdas, Lord of the Eorlin Heroes, Champion of the Thoroughfaire."

"*Aera!*" Thatch exclaimed out of silence, impressed.

"You are somebody, then," Mouse said, "A real somebody."

Haeseus was more confused than surprised, "When did he give you up?"

"He didn't," Iödas replied. "When they came for me, he refused them."

Mud scoffed, "I don't believe it. Nobody defends a bastard. Especially a Eorlin."

"He refused them," Iödas repeated, harder. "And then to keep my bloodline, his mistake, a secret, he slew the two soldiers who knew, who tried to take me by force. He buried them beneath our stables, Aerseusi."

"He must not have thought you a mistake, then," Haeseus said softly.

For a moment, Iödas thought Haeseus envied him, but Mud wasn't finished with his thought, "So, why are you here, fancy? If your father's so damned honorable with his dishonors."

"*Aera*, indeed," Iödas sighed, recalling the tourney grounds, but doing his best not to see the blow that sealed his fate for the hundredth time, "Whosoever knew I was a bastard then, whenever and wherever that secret found light again, they had been waiting. They must've hoped my father's interest would diminish, or protection vanish entirely with years. They waited a long time to no avail. Unfortunately for me, they fell into a bit of luck when my father fell on the fairegrounds, dead by a lance strike to the neck. They were there, and for all I know hired the man to take the mark, but they acted surely, without hesitation. And they sentenced me without trial, because that's what they do. I am no different than all of you."

"Except that you're a somebody," Mouse whispered.

Haeseus cocked his head – another question, "You gave no resistance?"

"I knew what I was."

"If you were his sole heir—" Thatch started.

Iödas interrupted, "I'm a bastard. We're heirs to nothing."

"Your mother?" Mouse asked.

"Call me an orphan as well, if you like."

"Did they kill her, too?" Mud asked, now heartedly caught in the tale.

"No. No, they didn't," Iödas looked past them, to the *Fyr-aeor Ritûm* far away, where the range that held Thorncrest joined with the Blackrock. With his silence held, came a silence from the rest of them. His despairingly wondrous tale had enthralled the company. They looked up to him now most-like, for the title he no longer bore, *but what's the use of that,* he thought?

As the prisoners crept closer to the mountains, the Fields of Eurymyr ebbed into barren rock, with little more than a narrow path to guide their slavers. The sun passed its blazing zenith, burning all in the cart by midafternoon. When the sun retreated, Thatch quietly gulped, fear in his eyes, "There she is."

Iödas squinted – Thorncrest rose on the distant horizon. With the Fields as flat as they were, a man could see for leagues, but it was terribly impossible to tell the physical distance of anything. It made it difficult to navigate, disheartening if you had a destination, and in this case Iödas couldn't help but wish it was a mirage. The mountain itself was not all that impressive as a landmass at this distance, the second shortest peak of the range, but he knew inside the deep would be deadly different.

Haeseus nudged Mouse awake, "You see that. The mines. That is where we are bound." He sighed, accepting this finality.

Mud grunted, "And that is where we will die."

The next two days were filled with each of the six slaves fading in and out of consciousness as their drivers didn't stop, whether for food or water or rest. The pair took six hour shifts and mumbled to each other all the way – this land, this sun, this trip was the only thing familiar to them. It was their life to haul others to their end, much like that of the *Ghisdain'rhil* bearing them down the river unto Shadow.

When they finally reached the foothills of the mountains, everyone on board was burned thrice over. If they weren't all about to be forgotten in the dark, Iödas would have cursed the sun, and if he'd known it was the last sunlight he'd see for the rest of his life, he may have taken the opportunity to appreciate it more; however, as it was, he swore to himself the black would not hold him ... in the end. When he saw the mines' foreboding entrance, held up by rotting timber, he mused it smaller than expected.

A large man with a large stick shoved them over the threshold – all six of them were weak and weary; any fight lay dormant within them – "Name's Burk. Whatever gods you worshipped before this day, forget them. I am your god now."

Dûnkrath be damned.

The company immediately found the tunnels reflected that of their entrance in the worst possible way. Iödas spotted shafts barely wide enough for Mouse to squeeze through, but when he saw the miners, he understood – they were malnourished beyond even the new recruits after three days of negligible sustenance; additionally, the slaves were forced to work through it, crawl wherefore when bidden, carve out deposits when presented, all to the point of exhaustion. They passed an elderly man miraculously still amongst the living, but he was pinned against a wall by Burk's enforcers; thongs of a braided leather lash whipped him relentlessly. Iödas said nothing, and couldn't care less what the man may have done to deserve such harsh punishment. He knew he would only join the elder if he so much as whispered to ask or raised a finger to help him.

The newly enslaved were shown to barebones quarters. Mouse was the only boy short enough to stand with any semblance of posture in the small cove; the rest were forced to bow their heads, and Haeseus strained to hunch over. Beyond the wooden door, a metal latch on its exterior, the cubical held a stone bed at each of the three walls, with a second bed existing less than two feet above it. Instead of wood-born and brought in, all six beds were shaved from the mine itself. One corner held a small, metal pot for waste, but the other corner was empty. There was no wasted coin here. It took a week for his eyes to adjust to the black, and another to adjust to the loss of time. Day broke when the foreman woke them; night fell when his company's shift was complete. The shifts consisted of thirteen hours of hard labor – finding a cavity, planting their feet, and chipping away at the rock with a small pick until the veins of ore surfaced to extract.

The metals he and the other slaves, orphans and bastards alike, unearthed were sent to a nearby village called Anvaer, whose sole purpose of existing was smelting the ore into armor sent south to ornament Oisin's Horselords. According to rumormongers, the town was one gargantuan smithy, but Iödas' imagination retraced his dreamsteps and thought of the promised land in his vision, an iron-wrought forge stronghold with a golden and garnet anvil at its center. However, there had to be more than that, because Anvaer also sent back one important ingredient to the slaves – oil for their lamps. The lamps tripled the shafts' heat in summer, and did little to warm them upon winter's arrival. Iödas was sure it was colder in the halls of black than outside on the Eurymyr, mantled in white by now, though he wasn't sure if he could remember the color of white as it were.

For eleven cycles of Aegis' twin moons, the six of them had made up a single cohesive team, and now they knew each other's every secret. For eleven cycles, they slaved away together drinking water poisoned by the very treasures they pursued. And for eleven cycles, they fed on horsemeat taken by the ill and dying draft horses, an old domesticated breed of equine out of Oisin's younger days. They were bred as beasts of burden who carried the ore to Anvaer every day. When their purpose on Aegis was done, they were still used, every part. Horses were all but worshipped by the Orsain equestrians, and never was a sacred steed wasted when the Shadow came calling. On occasion, Iödas slyly retrieved a hoof from the slaughter, and kept it for his own devise. He collected them, split them and made them as it were scales of mail. At the end of eleven cycles, a breastplate of bone sat in the corner their chambers, hidden from his new masters by intersecting bed slabs. He wore it on occasion under his thin scrap of linens to remind him of his father, who always fashioned his own plate instead of that which Anvaer set forth. Iödas never thought about it until he finished his own coat, but his father probably did it because he knew where the armor came from, who mined it, boys just like his own. Now, if his father were still alive, Iödas would be unrecognizable as the boy he was, a son-squire youth; instead, he was a man of scars left by fragments of limestone that pierced his cheeks and brow, fractured and let fly by his own swing. He was a man hardened, yet frail, and only passed his fourteenth nameday a slave in the dark.

Nearing the end of their twelfth cycle, Iödas, Mud, Thatch, Mute, Mouse, and Haeseus were assigned a mapping course. In actuality, little mapping was done on these assignments into the unknown; they simply found new pockets, new passages or thin walls to bring down in search of a new vein. Iödas woke with the urge to wear his mail that morning; it added a bit of warmth to this frozen nightmare, but he hoped it might bring him a bit of luck as well. On that day, it did, and he collected on a miracle.

His thoughts far from the mine, tapping along its dark walls attempting to recall the brilliance of the sun, he heard a faint, but sharp echo. He motioned, "Mud. Mouse. Over here."

The two friends closest joined him. Mud repeated the action with force and heard the ring of emptiness behind, "It's definitely comin' from the other side. Haeseus!"

His voice carried through the shaft; out of sight, the response called back, "What is it?"

"Fancy found something," Mud affirmed.

Haeseus arrived with Mute and Thatch, "Good or bad?"

Mud nodded to the wall, "We might get a thigh tonight."

Haeseus waved them all forward, "Good enough for me. Iödas?"

Iödas shrugged, "Let's hope it's easy."

As one, the company picked intersecting lines deep into the thin wall until Thatch punctured through. A pinhole of stale air exhaled into the shaft. Mouse held his lamp up to it, while Iödas peered in, "Definitely a pocket of something."

They chopped away until Mud got impatient, as he always did under any circumstance. Even after all this time with little food, he was the only one of them who stayed thick, retaining the same weight he'd arrived with. They all assumed he snuck extra meals somehow, and now were glad for it. He stepped back and ran shoulder first into the wall. With the force of his body, the web of cracks they cut caved entirely, and the wall collapsed; the others leapt back as Mud kept to the floor beneath the rubble. A rumbling resonance permeated the underground.

They all glanced around, unmoving. The dust settled, but they waited as the occasional pebble dropped to the floor, echoing with a nervous ripple through their cautious nature in the volatile shafts. However, in the end, there was no further consequence to his careless fervor.

"You're lucky that didn't cause a cave-in," Haeseus scolded.

"Then, we'd all be dead," Mud mused, looking up from where he lay in his own debris, "Where's the down side?"

Haeseus shook his head, "Iödas?"

Iödas took the first step over Mud, through the forced threshold, into a cavernous solutional hold, larger than any Thorncrest had ever produced for them in the past. When Iödas took the lamp from Mouse and lifted it, the light cast against the surrounding limestone sheened off at blinding angles, cascading across more than a dozen thick veins of naturally occurring quartz; however, the magnificence of its amaranthine hues told the story beneath – iron, and lots of it.

"Mouse, get Burk," Iödas called back. "Quickly."

The others entered and stood next to the son-squire in shock. Haeseus gawked, "This is incredible."

"There's a hundred suits of full plate in this pocket alone," Thatch added.

"Mute," Mud punched him on the arm lovingly, "If you're not mute, now's the time to say somethin'."

Mute said nothing.

Iödas paced along the perimeter of the chamber, analyzing. It was truly stunning, a glistening royal hall from his squiring days, his visit to the House of Oelar; bands leapt in purple waves across the stone. He understood why the Orsain Lords did what they did, sent the shame of society here to do what Kings could not – that's just the way things were. It was for the glory of their people to keep their culture pure. He shifted the mail beneath his tunic: *Could there be another way of life than this? Could banners fly for the orphans, a pennant for the bastards, as if they too were royalty?*

When the foreman arrived, he exclaimed, "*Aera!*" Burk rarely needed to speak at all, but when he did, it was pain that was delivered unconditionally; contrariwise, this time, he smiled a silver-toothed smile. None of them even knew he had teeth before that moment – it was a bad omen.

The next morning, Burk dropped a roll of plans in front of the mapping team. He wasn't the smartest man, but he was determined. And his brutish enforcers made sure he always got what he wanted. "Scaffolding – timber – running up the wall."

"But, why sir?" Haeseus asked bravely, "Shouldn't we get picking?"

Burk chuckled a deep, throaty bolster, "Go."

The uneducated party couldn't possibly understand his plan, chemically fortuitous in its speed as it would be, but Iödas saw through the devise. He'd more schooling in his years as his father's squire than Burk, his enforcers and the miners combined. Inevitably, Iödas knew the timber was only there to ignite.

It took half a shift to finish the scaffolding adjacent to the veins of ore. Three enforcers watched Iödas and his team every second of erection, which worried Iödas more than it ever had in the past. As they finished, Iödas spoke to each one of his friends in turn, "Rip off a long piece of your tunic and wrap it around your nose and mouth. This is going to get very bad, very quickly."

The enforcers laughed at this display and thrust torches into their hands when they returned to the threshold. "Now, light it," one said.

Iödas took his flaming brand first, knowing there wasn't much he could do, and led them to the wall. "Mud. Thatch. Mouse. Mute. Haeseus of the Aerseusi."

They all addressed him in turn, fear in their eyes.

"Start praying," Iödas finished.

They lit the timber together, and didn't know what hit them in the seconds that followed. The flames burst unexpectedly, incinerating Mud on impact. The others dove away, but the space was too confined and was black with smoke in seconds. They retreated in a chorus of coughs as the smoke filled their lungs, eyes burning hot as the fire that engulfed them. When they met with Burk's enforcers at the threshold, they were allowed no farther.

"You ain't goin' anywhere, slave," one spat at their feet. "Let's 'ave some fun."

The fire gained in strength behind them as if the very sun was closing on their backs. "Mud's already dead," Iödas challenged.

"Who cares," Burk interrupted, joining his enforcers at the threshold. He had a strange contraption covering his own mouth, feeding a tube of sorts to a cylinder on his back – he knew exactly what would happen, but wasn't finished. "Go get the buckets, lads." His enforcers left to retrieve Burk's orders.

The flames licked at the limestone, and Iödas saw the flesh on the nape of Thatch's neck begin to boil. However, when he looked at the others, they perceived something else – Burk was alone.

With the fire reflecting devils in his eyes, Burk saw the fire in theirs, "I wouldn't if I were you."

"There's five of us and one of you," Thatch moved forward.

Without hesitation, Burk kicked out, landing a heel into Thatch's kidney, sending him tumbling backward to the scalding floor. He cried out as he rolled across it, skin peeling off to bare muscle and bone. He tried to rise, but the smoke enveloped him and before he could make it back to the threshold, his lungs were overcome and asphyxiated. He dropped dead behind Mouse.

"There's one of me. And you are nothing," Burk declared.

"You didn't have to do that," Mute whispered.

Iödas, Haeseus, and Mouse spun on their heels.

"Did you just—?" Mouse started, but Mute had already attacked. His pick dug into Burk's arm, who only gritted his teeth and pulled Mute toward him, between the others and himself in case he needed the barrier. They heard Mute's wrist snap over the crackling hiss of flames. It was as if a pit of vipers was behind them and a lone *baerborr* stood in front of them.

Burk lifted the boy off the floor and used his other hand to reach behind his back. He produced a large hunting knife. "I will not have insurrectionist rats in my den." He gutted and dropped Mute to the floor. The others stared at the body of the poor boy, but said nothing. It wasn't long before he disappeared in the smoke filling the hold. It was thickening, and leaking into the outer shafts of the tunnel.

When his enforcers returned with buckets, Burk shoved three in the remaining hands off the slaves, but left three with his enforcers as Mud and Mute and Thatch were all gone.

Iödas looked down and saw the bucket was filled with water and a dust of some sort he didn't recognize, but understood. "It will erupt."

"I'm an impatient man," Burk smiled.

The enforcers pushed them back into the death awaiting them in the poisoned pocket. The enforcers themselves spread out, but had no protection against the smoke. One keeled over before he reached his post and the contents of his bucket spilled across the floor, wasted. The other two held their ground as best they could.

"Now!" Burk screamed, though it was barely audible above the roar of immolation.

Iödas knew waiting was not an option in this heat, so they blindly tossed the buckets of liquid across the rock face simultaneously. A series of explosions caused by thermal shock and whatever else resided in the water detonated through the veins in the wall, cracks that had been split open by the fire in the past half hour. All was ignited and all blasted apart in seconds.

Iödas dove into Mouse, pushing him away from a large chunk of rock amongst innumerable others in the avalanche. The ceiling, or at least part of it, was caving in due to the basic loss of structure. The boulder that should've taken Mouse's life instead struck Iödas' shoulder, but glanced off his coat of mail beneath – it could've easily sheared his whole arm away if it wasn't for his makeshift plate. Burk's remaining enforcers weren't so lucky: One was caught in the initial blast, while another was speared through the skull by a large piece of ore. Iödas, Mouse, and Haeseus leapt through the threshold as one to the outer shaft, on either side of

Burk, landing hard on the burning stone floor below the smoke line.

Burk hadn't moved an inch. Iödas stayed flat on the floor with his arms covering his friends' necks, theirs his, until all signs of the collapse subsided.

Burk took a deep breath through the strange tube feeding him what must've consisted of purified air of some sort. "It's ready," Burk stepped over his slaves.

When the smoke cleared, Iödas, Haeseus, and Mouse finally rose one by one. They turned and saw thousands of veins exposed, and as much and more in the rubble littering the ruin of the cave. Thatch was right, this hall alone could supply enough ore to armor the entire mining society helm to spur. The explosion had completed years of individual labors.

If only the others hadn't acted so prematurely. Iödas whispered, "It's time."

"Time for what?" Haeseus asked lowly.

Burk stood at the remains of the wall, a deep bowl hewn through its center. He ran his hands lightly along the exposed veins, its purity mesmerizing.

Yes, Iödas thought, *it is time.* He walked up behind Burk. "Milord, foreman?"

Burk couldn't take his eyes off the shimmering wall, "Yes, slave?"

Iödas studied the ground, found a sharp piece of haematite and picked it up, careful and soundless.

"Iödas, no!" Haeseus snapped from the threshold.

Iödas whispered in Burk's ear, who was far too gone to recognize Haeseus' plea, "Would you like to look me in the eyes as I kill you, or would you like to keep staring into our veins."

It took a long moment for Burk to process the statement, far longer than it should have; nevertheless, Burk finally spun on his heels. When his eyes met the bastard Eorlin's, his throat was already draining dry, slit from end to end as he turned.

Iödas rejoined Haeseus at the threshold – Mouse was gone.

"What is this, Iödas?" he asked in shock.

"We've lived far too long in this eternal night. Now, it's time we welcome the dawn." He placed his hand on his friend's shoulder and squeezed, "It's time to leave."

They entered the central shaft together and saw Mouse standing in wait. The workers stopped working when they spotted the piece of haematite in Iödas' hand, Burk's blood still warm on its glistening edge. The enforcers attempted to push the slaves back to their endless picking, but no one moved. One guard turned to the lash, but its victim cared little, while another moved toward Iödas. The slaves knew exactly what this was, what it meant, and so did the enforcers – a revolution.

Mouse was the first to launch himself on the brute in mid thrash, and all others followed suit without hesitation. Many died in the shaft that day, slaves and masters alike, but in the end, the numbers were all that mattered. The miners outnumbered their enforcers four-to-one. In no time at all, the mineshaft was stained a deep carmine, its limestone tainted garnet, barely noticeable in the black, before Iödas led his followers away from the newly bowelled tomb silently, through the upper core of Thorncrest. Anyone in their path was swiftly removed, slain silent and unnoticed – no one knew the dark as they, the slaves, the daemons of the pits as they were.

When the light of the sun struck their eyes within the entrance shaft, many lost their breath, some fell to the ground, but all found their spirit renewed; some gasped, others cried, but all shut their eyes to the strength of day, and all gave thanks to the Wrath or Valorlord. However, Iödas held out his hand to stay his little army before they could exit, "Wait," he said. "We are blinded. We must adjust to the angelic when leaving the sup of devils."

They waited patiently, respectfully, without word there at Thorncrest's access for hours until their retinas no longer burned with freedom, until the soil without came into focus clearly. Then, as the sun set, they heard a cart crunching across the northern Eurymyr. "Another barrow," Haeseus conjectured.

"Six more damned," another returned.

"Today, they find forgiveness," Mouse added.

"Keep to the Shadow," Iödas asserted.

The miners kept to the shaft's entrance and listened; the wagon creaked and cracked closer across the roughening terrain. "Burk!" one of the soldiers called out from his driver's seat. "Burk, get your rusted flankies out here! We got another six for ya!"

When no one responded, the Oisin soldier hopped off the cart and stepped through the shaft's threshold. Before his next step, he was already face down in a pool of his own blood. Iödas motioned the miners forward, and when they emerged into the fading light of the setting sun, the warmth caught them by surprise. It was winter, and snow mantled the earth, but the last rays washed over their faces, an embracing quilt of mercy from their gods.

The remaining guard atop his seat attempted to whip the horses into motion, but the miners surrounded it and the beasts pranced in place. "What are you doing, slaves?" he demanded, a younger lad than most in his service. "Where's the foreman?"

Iödas stepped forward, "I see no slaves here. We are free men. And these are our mines. Were you under some other assumption?" He climbed up to the seat and plopped down next to the golden-haired youth; meanwhile, the miners freed the six passengers. One of those newly appointed reached for the driver's throat, but Iödas pushed him back, "No. He lives." He pressed the shard of haematite against the man's collar, trailing it down his chest and pricking it through his leathers to cut into his sternum. A drop of blood straggled down its shaft and between Iödas' scarred fingers. "What's your name?"

The response came with a stammer, "Orsiryn."

Iödas raised a brow, "That's an heirborne name. What are you doing way out here, Orsiryn?"

"My... My mother's on the Thatched Council. Vicar of the Thoroughbred. This was ... an opportunity to see another side of our world, to witness our shame, so I may not make the mistake of lesser men."

"Of lesser men? In the hope that you, in your frail boyhood, would not sire a thing like us in some vain attempt to prove your coming of age? I see. Well, I hope I haven't disappointed you, Orsiryn. But, what an experience for you, eh?!" Iödas cried out with a smile, startling the youth, but bolstering his men with chuckles. Many coughs proceeded this; it was a long time for all since laughter escaped their lips.

Iödas removed the mineral blade from his adversary's chest and wrapped his arm around Orsiryn's shoulders casually, "Go back to your Horselords, heirborne errand-boy. Tell them Thorncrest is liberated. These forges are lit for those that bled for them, here at Orphan's End."

"They... They'll kill you all."

"They will try."

"You're starting a war."

"The war started long ago."

Iödas leapt from the cart, but before Orsiryn could crack the reins, he turned back, "Oh, I almost forgot." He freed the weary horse from its binds to the barrow, a white mare with a mane of black, as pitch as the ore they delved, "She's no slave either. You walk back."

Orsiryn fumbled off the bench without further prompt and fell from the cart. The miners chortled and watched the youth race across the Fields of Eurymyr until he disappeared in the fall of night.

Haeseus and Mouse were at Iödas' side. "You want them all dead?" Haeseus asked.

"No. Of course not," Iödas replied.

"We want equality. Peace," Mouse understood.

"What about Anvaer?" Haeseus questioned the stronghold to the east.

"We raze it asunder. And Orphaeon will rise from its ashes."

Anthology I

A Bayman's Burden

Dyn Kaird, Cabin Boy

The Embers

The Silent Sea

*...being a short story during the Age of Origin,
approximately in the year 706...*

Dyn Kaird waited for his master's return. The sun scorched his brow as he watched a light wind nip through the tattered sails above him, furled at harbor. The fading linen dreamt of the night the backstay secured them lovingly to the mast's summit at berth, before years of hunting and piracy weathered them worn and weary. The white was now a Shadow of such, soot-stained reaching black at her leech. She was riddled with patches, remnant holes left by cannon fire mended haphazardly during battle due to necessity, instead of aesthetic appeal. They never had time for that. So many were left abandoned unto decay, much like the symptoms of her bulkheads. The planks of the deck bowed, the railing bent, and the masts themselves had seen worse days than their colors. The timber was rotting, and mold no longer hid in the damp of her cellars, but festered along anything its reach latched onto. It was a lover, lecherous in its labor and taxing in its atrophy. Dyn knew the *Bighter's Wrath* sailed her last leagues during the Reignwalker's Civil War. If that brutal example of bloody misunderstanding wasn't enough to drown them, they were sure to perish on whatever journey lay ahead. *Why can't we just be done*, Dyn thought sadly.

Dyn was thin for a Bayman, most of his culture thick, hairy, and heavily scarred. His fiery red hair was all he had to mark him a Bighter true. His smaller stature was owed to a lineage that betrayed him, blood only half Bayman, the other half their enemy. His mother was of seafaring folk certainly, but died giving birth, so his younger years were spent with his ill-gotten drunk of a father across the Eventyr Bight, until the Reignwalking sod fell off his own ship and drowned, all while surrendering to the *Wrath*. Dyn was lucky – it was his ninth nameday, and the captain of the *Wrath* pitied his lot; not to mention, the man's previous cabin boy was killed only hours earlier in a tide-line skirmish. The next six years of Dyn's life was sworn over to the *Wrath's* service – he behaved, never asked questions, never talked back, and did what he was told without too much thought on the matter. Maybe that struck others as lacking character, but his character could resurface once they all retired rich men and weren't facing death every day of their war-torn lives. In truth, that fighting was over now, the Coastal Treaty to be signed during the next cycle's highest tide, so Dyn knew something had to be wrong. He felt it on the wind. *Why are we waiting?*

Sweat dripped down his forearm and ran through his fingers to the railing he held tighter than if it were *syn*. He kept his eyes scanning the streets of the Fyrzain harbor. The city was a bustling town along the Eventyr Bight, on anyone's way to the Embers capital – Ildûron. In fact, if the tales were true, Fyrzain was erected as a prison for Ildûron's traitors during the Emberkings War over three hundred years ago. When the war was over, the prisoners were all but forgotten and left in the city, its new citizens. The buildings kept, and a government was roughly hammered into a society; it was raw, and law was rarely adhered to, but the city functioned, and they answered to Ildûron in the end. The entire city was the color of pitch, the stone black from the *Fyr-aeor Ritûm*, and the timbers blackened in some fashion when erected; it was a fact now that no one would forget where the people came from – an ominous, disparaging past. Given all that, the folk at present were kindly as any brigand could ask for.

A flock of gray *lanser* flew by screeching, circling the *Wrath's* masts in chase of one another until they shot off to the next warren of sails. They were pesky avians, always stealing bread from the market tables along the pier. One ship, ironically registered *The Gull*, had been sitting at dock so long, each of its three crow's nests sported overly tangled lanser nests. The crow lost an eye to one of the mothers, but had quite the feast that night. They were still attempting to clear out the other two. When Dyn's eyes, both currently residing healthily in their sockets, returned to the bustling wharfs, he saw his master sprinting down the lane with the strides of a giant. The trade was heavy during the morning, and it was a miracle that of the grace his brute of a captain displayed avoiding the cross traffic. After all, his stride was not the only aspect of him akin to an *ogri*.

Captain Byrbor Fire-Guzzler, or more recently renown as Byrbor Bed-Breaker, was in fine shape for a man in his latter years, eating nothing but the meat and flower provided by the sea. He towered over the rest of the Fyrzain commons, dodging past them with nimble ease. He was a pirate lord as it were now, and his crew trusted him. They'd suffered greatly together through the war, calling him Fire-Guzzler for a reason. Ship after enemy ship burned under the cannons of the *Wrath*; afterward, Byrbor would order the helm straight through the wreckage. Bed-Breaker was used thereafter, as he recently committed a slue of crusades against the married men of the Bight, breaking their beds during friendly bouts with their wives. Many second story windows were broken as well.

It was no one's place aboard to judge the captain on his moral antics; they judged him solely on the greatness of his deeds and depth of his treasures. Byrbor was a man of action, not words. Bed-Breaker's vernacular was limited to rather unimaginative descriptions of affection and the five hundred or so seafaring terms needed to captain his vessel with authority absolute. At present, Byrbor leapt over the rail of his vessel and grabbed Dyn by the arm, "Let's go, boy."

Captain Byrbor threw Dyn into his cabin and moved to a central table where maps and charts of the Silent Sea's coast were detailed in technique oddly intricate for a man who couldn't read. The rest of the cabin was as lavish as always in the only reason it needed to be; consequently, there were no chairs, only pillowed surfaces billowing with feather and fur, layers of the finest silks, warmest wools, and most expensive pelts from across the Realms of Aegis. The first room Byrbor would pillage on any given vessel taken at sea would not be the hold, or room of treasury, but the captain's cabin. The personal effects of a captain are what told his story, and his wealth.

The captain wiped the table clean with one swift clearing by his massive arm, the works of guidance clattering to the floor carelessly. With the other, he reached into his ornately woven and intricately embroidered overcoat – the frays and stains of years at sea did nothing to diminish its grandeur, fine and flamboyant. He drew from it a rolled-up parchment, thin and crackling with age. Contrary to his overzealous demeanor, a calm set over withdrawing it. He snipped the knot from the thong that tied it cylindrically, and smoothed it out, pressing it flat across the table with a deft attention.

At every crease, at every touch, there was risk of breaking apart the withering page, but for Byrbor's strength, he could also be gentle. He nodded at the weights now floored, which Dyn retrieved and placed at the parchment's corners cautiously. His master asked quietly, "D'ya see anything?"

Dyn eyed the paper warily. *A trick question, is it?* he thought. He saw nothing, the surface was blank. Fear gripped him and held his tongue.

"Well?!" the captain surged.

"No, sir," Dyn stuttered, "I'm sorry."

"Fer what?" the captain smiled.

"I..." Dyn caught himself, "No, sir, I don't see anything," he reaffirmed confidently.

"*Aera!*" Byrbor exclaimed, "I knew ya wouldn't lie to me, boy."

Dyn waited. He knew his master would expand on this mystery if he needed to know. However, as it was, it appeared he didn't.

"Go fetch m'first," Byrbor commanded, a twinkle in his eye.

Dyn immediately exited the cabin to retrieve Tisdon, the *Bighter's Wrath's* quartermaster.

The weather deck was empty – everyone ashore on leave. Dyn poked his head below, into the hold, and scanned its halls at the crossroads. The cook, Kreel, was the only one in sight, chopping onions in the galley. At the sight of Dyn's thick red locks falling into view, the boisterous behemoth bellowed, "Dyn, m'boy! Ya goin' ashore, 'en?"

"'Ave ya see Tisdon, sir?"

"Don't think so," his jowls flapped from side to side. "Then again, can't rightly see ma feet."

"Then, yes. Seems I'm going ashore, sir."

"A bushel o' *garsoni,* 'en, and a salt brick, will ya, lad?"

"Aye, sir."

Dyn removed himself from the hold. He was as much a servant to the rest of the crew as he was to his master, but he didn't mind. They treated him well enough as anyone in his position deserved. After all, he was a cabin boy, which meant servant when one is acquired from an enemy vessel as bounty. They only beat him when he really mucked up.

It didn't take long to pick up the *garson* fruits and salt block, and he carried them both in a large, stretched-to-its-thinnest-seam pouch at his side for hours as nightfall came to Fyrzain's haunting scape. He finally located Tisdon in the first place he should've looked – one of two dozen cemeteries between prison quads.

The cemetery was five hundred feet square, surrounded by the tall, black buildings that ruled the city's rise; the structures were built precisely high enough for one purpose – no matter where the sun was located in the sky, the graves of each deathblock were kept in Shadow. Even at midday, they were dark, though Dyn could never figure out how. Currently, the twin moons of Aegis were choked out by a starless night of clouds promising rain, not uncommon for the season. The minimal light that escaped their clutches cast an eerie glow on the ghostly glade.

The quartermaster, Tisdon, was a man well-kempt for one of his trade and culture, and the only vagabond aboard who spent his time ashore in anyplace other than the nearest brothel. The rest of the swabs anchored at the closest silk house to the harbor to crack Jeneny's teacup in local delight. Contrariwise, Tisdon knelt at the grave of his wife, but heard Dyn's footsteps as he approached. "'Ello, Kaird," he greeted without turning. He was the only one aboard who used Dyn's surname rather than his accustomed 'boy'. Dyn was never sure why.

Dyn stopped a few feet behind his superior, "Cap'n's lookin' for ya, sir."

"How long?" Tisdon asked.

"Few hours, now."

"He's lost in drink, I'm sure."

"Most-like. He's excited 'bout somethin'."

"Fer *'zhri's* sake," Tisdon sighed, evidently as exhausted as Dyn of the seafaring life.

"It's ... strange," Dyn thought to explain, but couldn't find the words.

Tisdon rose, but kept his eyes on the mound, "Steppin' back aboard means another trip into the Silence."

"She ain't got more 'an a drift left in her, if ya don't mind ma 'pinion, sir." Dyn knew the quartermaster never did.

"She'll hold on calm waters well enough. But, another battle, or worse – a storm... Aye, we'll sink to the bottom of the Deep on the morrow in that case."

As if on cue, lightning struck, and drops of rain pelted the tombstones surrounding them.

Were the dead crying? Or calling for them? Thunder rumbled a low and thrumming moan across the darkening sky.

Tisdon placed his hand on the grave. "Ya don't have to be so pushy, love. I'll see ya soon."

Kaird and Tisdon returned to the harbor, but the quartermaster ordered the cabin boy to round up the rest of the crew, while he went aboard. As expected, Dyn found them all in the Derelict Daughter. It took a few hours, but eventually the sailors, gunners, and boatswains sobered up and exited their curtained quarters. Dyn was forced to wrap his arm around the crow of the nest, Fornos, and lead him personally from the harbor up the *Wrath's* gangplank to drop him off against the closest square rigging. He found the oil lamps of Byrbor's cabin burning low, but retreated to his own small cell in the *Wrath's* belly to await further orders.

Unlike the rest of the crew quarters, which were double or triple bunked, his compartment was all his own – a cabin boy's only privilege. A miniscule porthole allowed a glimpse of the starlight beyond, thin rays breaking through the storm clouds whenever they could manage a peek. Dyn found the constellation Lûmlaeris, shining brighter than any other. Its guiding light led any sailor toward the Zhrizûr Divide, which primarily coincided with north, unless one was all the way up through the glaciers along the Frostcrags – uncharted territory. Dyn's eyes burned as he laid back in the netting he called a bed, using his foot to sway back and forth as the waves would at sea, reminiscent of a tidal lullaby. He craved to find Somnyr in the black, but he couldn't let the mantles of sleep take him tonight. Not yet.

Tonight, Dyn waited. He stared at a small, brass bell nailed into the crossbeam overhead his hammock. A string led to Byrbor's cabin, a deck above, in three places – wherever the captain lay, he could easily call for his boy.

Another hour passed, and it grew harder and harder to stay attentive, the lapping of the water against the dock a lulling of the Silent Sea pushing him to dream. As his eyes fluttered, their weight unmanageable, the clang of the bell shattered the cabin's calm – it rang out three times. Dyn would've only heard the first, had he not tripped over his hammock's mesh, falling face first to the floorboards. He scrambled up and out the door as fast as his weary state could muster.

When Dyn reached the captain's cabin, he didn't bother to knock. Byrbor told him day one, if he wanted his boy, his boy entered. The captain loathed waiting.

Upon entering, Dyn was nearly knocked over by Byrbor passing him by and out the door, "Bring the table, boy." It took Dyn a moment to process. He saw Tisdon staring out the large bay window that made up the entire rear of the cabin.

While Dyn folded up the collapsible table, he couldn't help but wonder why the quartermaster hadn't followed his captain. "Sir?" Dyn called across the expanse, permeated with fear and disappointment, "Are ya comin'?"

"Go ahead, Kaird. I know all I need to of Byrbor's madness."

Dyn didn't understand, but finished collecting up the table and closed the door behind him. He ascended the quarterdeck and reset the surface. The queer sight of it brought many of the crew to the scene without warrant. Others were brought by whispers and curiosity. Byrbor sat on the aft rail until everyone was gathered without call. He reveled in the anticipation. After minutes of unbridled fidgeting, he hopped down. He called out as clearly as he could, as if in testimony to the gods, and his hand dashed into his overcoat, "I have in my hand, the discovery of a lifetime!"

Yup. They were doing it again. The rain fell harder, rising with Byrbor's heat. Dyn wondered why they couldn't have done this in the hold ... or in the morning. It was a blank piece of paper for Elzhri's sake.

"There are legends," Byrbor continued, "of the great and mysterious Elvar who dwell in the mountains north of us. Some worship 'em like gods, but are they such? Fer reading the stars and forecasting futures? I have in my hand the key to their secrets. It will lead us to their deepest cove along the *ritûm*, written in the sacred letters of the Elvar's cryptic guise. They cannot be read by mortal eyes, they say. But, under the right circumstances..."

Byrbor waited, allowing this to sink in. Now, everyone wanted to know. He was always so good at this.

"They say, when the tears of the *Evar'tûm* fall 'cross Aegis, the words of Elvar prophecy reveal themselves. I test that theory tonight; I challenge that legend in front of you all. We see nothin', we're done. Retire with the wealth the *Wrath* brought ya, and I will live out my last days on her deck, dreamin' of our glory days from this prisoner's harbor. But, if I'm right, our journey has one last league in its sail. And we will live, not as nobles, but as kings! With the wonders of the Elvar borne about our necks, shining from our fingers, draped over our shoulders, we'll walk like gods among men!"

The crew erupted in applause and cheers of surmounting desire. Alongside them, other crews had woken, and were peering out of their portholes at the intrigue rising in the dead of night. It was a great proposition; however, Dyn's support was empty, hollow in the knowledge that another fight would be mocking death and daring the Shadow to take them one too many times. How many others felt the same? How many others prayed to the Eleven True that what lay secret in the captain's coat was a forgery?

They held their breath as Byrbor removed the scroll. It was immediately soaked in the downpour as he unrolled it, and the night was suddenly alight with a striking glow of a thousand little beams glistening from the parchment where its letters and lines were brought to life. It was rumored the Elvar wrote in a mystical ink, a gem crushed to dust and mixed alchemically with an oil found only in the mountains of the *Evar-aeor* – it was invisible to mortal eyes, unless wet with their tears, they said. It seemed that rumor was true; unfortunately, that kind of secret held consequences. The parchment broke apart on each droplet's impact, and Byrbor howled in triumph, "Ho! Take it in, lads! Remember it, all of you!"

Dyn stared at the beauteous illumination. The lines traced the boundaries of the Elvar's home, and the depths of the tunnels and coves impossible to maneuver and navigate without this map. He found himself quickly forgetting about the dread end of certain possibilities, and saw only the fortune, the fame. This truly was the greatest discovery in Baymen history. And they would live like Kings, if just one more tale of the Elvar proved true – the cryptic riches of their coves.

When the parchment was gone, disintegrated beyond saving and blown away, Byrbor addressed his men again. "We set sail immediately, we can't wash away an ounce of memory in the rivers of sleep, perchance to lose it in dream."

The next moment was pure chaos – the boatswains ran to their posts, the crow fumbled up to his nest, the sails were dropped and their dimming flags unfurled. Anchor was hoisted from its bed, and the rope lines cast back to the harbor's ties. They were off – to roils and riches, or one or the other.

Their sails quickly made headway from the Gulf of Ilsûri, rounded the tip of the Eventyr Bight and pushed through the cross current gales to greet open sea. The storm worsened as they speared northward along the Silent Coast. Lightning flashed and thunder boomed an awakening of wrath against *Wrath*. The skies and the sea worked as one to throw the *Bighter* off her course, but her crew was ready and held steadfast to their talents.

A league away from the *Evar-aeor's* borders, they hit the reefs. The ridging banks that dipped and rose, jutted out and slipped away along the *ritûm* were treacherous enough for a warship, let alone their limited brigantine. The mountain range itself fell directly into the waves and there was no shoreline to be had. Along the rim, through the storm, Dyn spotted countless wrecks half drowned – clippers to dreadnoughts, frigates to man-o-wars, watched them with haunting hulls waiting for another to join their masses. Dyn lost track of time, but was sure dawn had come and gone, while the storm kept the sky black and waves blacker.

Sscraaaack!

The *Wrath* scraped along something not far enough below the tides, and everyone heard the deafening rupture. Shouts from below were drowned by the slashing winds. Dyn shot a glance to Byrbor, who motioned to the hold, "Go, boy!"

Dyn sprinted down the quarterdeck, grabbed the rail to steady himself, but slipped on the steps down and tumbled forward. One of the riggers on the weather deck caught him, but the ship jerked and sent the poor soul over the starboard banister. There was no use searching the sea, the Deep had taken its first victim.

Dyn dove into the hold and splashed to the floor. Three inches of water was present and rising. Three men attempted to stave off the advance of rushing tides into the belly of the *Bighter*, but to no avail. The reef had punctured a foot-wide hole through her keel – they were sinking.

There was a magnificent crack that resounded over the roaring hell, and a scream followed. Dyn spun on his heels and spotted Fornos out the nearest porthole splash into the tidal abyss. Three feet from Dyn, the crow's nest crashed through the weather deck into the galley. Splinters shed and shot out in every direction. Three men were killed on the crushing impact, while another two caught shards of it like arrows through temple and spine. Dyn screamed in pain, falling to his knees in the mirk – his leg was gashed bloody, but not rent through. He forced his way up the steps and out of the hold, leaving behind a trailing river of red to join the unfortunate souls caught under the collapse.

They were scoring the reefs along the roots of the mountains now, drawing ever closer to a maw of spiraling black crags that rose from the Deep north of them. Byrbor roared, "Blimey! I see it! Thar, off the bow – three cables!"

Sure enough, three hundred fathoms in front of them, through the dark spires, there was illumination revealing the cove's nature, a faint glow that welcomed fools into the maw. *We'll never make it past her teeth,* Dyn thought.

The mainsail was gone, and the crew was haphazardly attempting to draw the mizzenmast under control. At first, they succeeded, but then a rushing wind snapped its lines and the yardarm swung down, smashing into Byrbor before it tore away and flipped into the sea. The captain fell hard to the floorboards of the quarterdeck, a heap of broken bones, but crawled his way to the helm, who's swab was nowhere in sight. Most of the men could no longer tend their duties, and chaos reigned over the *Wrath.* Where was Tisdon?

Instead of returning to his master, Dyn rushed into the captain's cabin. The bay window was shattered, and the tempest lashed through the cabin. Tisdon was still in attendance, lying across the plush lavishness of his captain's luxury.

"We're sinkin'!" Dyn cried.

"Let me raise up my arms, and I'll lift us to the *Evar'tûm.*" Tisdon had gone as mad in despair as Byrbor was in adventure.

"We need you," Dyn pleaded.

Tisdon waved the cabin boy over, who stumbled to his side. The quartermaster snatched Dyn's collar and pulled him close, staring into his eyes, darting one to the other, "Listen to me, Kaird. Never thought ya obeyed outta stupidity. He's had a death wish fer sometime, now. Will ya sign for it? Join us in the Deep?"

"What're ya talkin' about?"

Tisdon drew him closer, "Take care of yer family when it comes, cap'n. Better 'an we took care of you."

The ship reared through an incoming squall. The quartermaster and cabin boy toppled over and slid down across the tipping floor toward the nonexistent window. Dyn grabbed a piece of frame securely welded into the stern; it gouged into his hand, but stopped his descent. Tisdon didn't even try. He welcomed the black that swallowed him whole.

Dyn held tight to the stern, and realized it was easier to ascend that way, climb over the aft rail to the quarterdeck, than attempt to crawl back into the cabin. He took one step at a time, hand over bloody hand. Time stood still for his thoughts to race through Tisdon's words. Even if they found their way to the cove, and miraculously found some rocky shoreline, what then? Byrbor was mad with venture, lost to the lust of unnecessary wealth.

Even if they returned as Kings, Byrbor would always need more.

Dyn pulled himself to the quarterdeck, where he found his captain gripping the wheel tightly with one hand, while another held his ribs. Dyn could see blood dripping out of Byrbor's buckles and flooding strands through his fingers. The cabin boy joined his master to help steady the wheel. The Bed-Breaker smiled a golden-toothed smile, "That's m'boy."

In the shape they found themselves in, a single mast and a crew half drowned, the crags of the cove's maw came upon them incredibly fast. They scored the sides of the first spires, but pressed through the cranny of death. The next pair were too close together, and sheared the cannons on the port side. The stern, being wider than the rest of the ship, caught against the rocks and twisted them about in their forward speed. The crags crumbled over them, many of them pounding across the deck in a lethal stone rain. Byrbor was struck down by the largest of the falling boulders; intuitively, Dyn levered himself against the freed wheel in an attempt to steady them. This was it. The cove was less than thirty yards away, but far too small for them to enter. There was no hope in anchoring, but they wouldn't survive a collision at this speed. Dyn spun the wheel as hard as he could to port, the rudder miraculously intact, and they slammed into the mountainside afore the breach.

The *Bighter's Wrath* brought down rock and tree in a mudslide across the decks – if they were to die, they'd leave a scar. Forthright, the tactic succeeded; they slowed, but there was no stopping. There was still far too much force behind her. The *Wrath* pivoted back neutral and headstrong into the cove's entrance. The bowsprit struck the roof of the cove and dug into it; accordingly, a shocking jolt of halted momentum threw the remaining crew forward. Instead of snapping; however, the bowsprit held, which pushed the stern of the ship down into the water, inverting her at an angle into the Deep. The crew tumbled back the way they came. Many attempted to grab onto whatever odds and ends they could, but the rush of water flooded over them, and all were lost. Dyn never let go of the helm, but the wheel snapped away, and brought him with it in its descent through the vortex of aqueous ruin.

Dyn awoke to the sound of a *lanser* flock's caws as they circled over the dead like vultures. His eyes fluttered open and squinted. The light of the sun shone through wisps of clouds that revealed no trace of the storm. He coughed, choked, and rolled over. He hacked and spit up until the taste of salt water lingered no longer on his tongue, and crawled to a shallow pool of fresh water nearby to wash his cracked lips. Every muscle ached, every joint popped, but he tilted his head up to survey his surroundings. He survived on a low escarpment of rock jutting out from the cove at its entrance. The remains of the *Bighter's Wrath* were strewn over the waters of the reef, a cul-de-sac of ruin. The *Wrath's* bowsprit still resided in the cove's palate, and the ship was half-sunk at a forty-five-degree angle beneath the waters of the reef, stained by oil, powder, and blood. It didn't look like she'd split in two, but she was far from salvageable. She was buried, and would never sail again. The *Bighter's Wrath* was no more, and her crew perished.

"Heh! He's alive, boys."

Dyn whirled around, and instantly regretted it – every nerve shocked with displeasure, and nausea set in. He swallowed hard to keep what little morsels were left in his stomach down, then saw a ring of mates across the platform who'd survived. They'd already pulled a few crates of rations ashore, well-enough intact, and lay across them, bathing in the sunlight. Dyn rose, groaning, and cut to the chase in greeting them, "The captain?"

Marryk, the master gunner, shook his head, "Gone. Thought you were dead, too, boy."

"Thought we'd have to eat ya at week's end," Kreel guffawed. How the obese chef of urchins lived, Dyn didn't dare muse.

"Looks like ya've got plenty to survive 'ere," Dyn joined them, perching atop a crate of *yari*.

"Survive? How long?" It was a rigger called Razor whose hopes were abandoned.

Dyn stared into the cove. The faint glow spotted the night before shone from the cove at least a mile in.

Marryk shook his head, "Well, fellas, there's a dinghy out there – ya see it? Looks like it survived. S'pose it's time to fumble our way back home."

"No," Dyn rejected.

All three stared at him, incredulous.

Dyn kept his eyes on the depths of mystery. It enthralled him, drew him in, yet warned him to keep out, or pay the price. "I thought we came to steal somethin'."

"It's over, boy," Marryk refused.

"I sure ain't goin' in thar," Kreel reinforced.

"Oh, c'mon, boys," Dyn addressed them as equals now, for there was no captain, no quartermaster, no law. "Was this fer nothin'? Did our mates die for naught? Don't ya wonder what the Elvar keep hidden away in their dark halls? What secrets hold 'em so high above us? Sure, they read the stars, if tales be true, but what does that make 'em? Gods-like? Nay! More like glorified librarians! I say we take their mysteries and reveal 'em to the world. What are we, after all?"

There was a moment's pause. "Pirates?" Kreel offered, confused.

"Exactly!" Dyn cried out, startling his mates. "Our fate and our fortune is our own, not theirs, and not the sea's. It didn't take us last night; it won't take us on the morrow. We're goin' through these mountains, and comin' out on the other side as kings!"

The three survivors sitting in their circle of futility stared at him as if he were mad. *Maybe I am,* he thought. *Byrbor died for this. But, now we have nothing, and I can't let us go home empty-handed. Not after all that's happened. We're meant to do this...*

It was Kreel who bolstered again in a heaving bellow, "A'right, Cap'n Kaird. Lead the way."

An Elvar's Edict

Evendir Ko Ûrotyr

Evar-aeor Ritûm

...being a short story during the Age of Origin, approximately in the year 706...

Evendir Ko Ûrotyr watched in vigilant fascination, captivated by the ridiculous wreck of Baymen, who now scoured their own ruin, a sacrilegious folly, for supplies. Their warship's collision had scored the *Lûmrhik'aeon*, and these survivors should be punished. But, how?

From her vantage – the shelf of a cliff face rising from the Bay of Lûm – she'd watched the whole catastrophic incident and grew more impressed with each new body that floundered ashore alive. She saw four of them now, mere silhouettes in the morning mists, their voices drowned by the lapping tides against the reef. They found a dinghy intact and filled it with provisions. While they appeared persistent, the devils wouldn't make it far into the Sanctuary of Light with the intelligence of pirates. Within the hour, the figures drifted into the cove on the shifting currents through the wreck-riddled crags, and the black engulfed them. Evendir dropped from her perch to the brink of a lower escarpment to follow. She slipped through a crack in the mountain wall and disappeared to track the *Lûmrhik's* courseway.

Evendir shifted easily down the claustrophobic cranny. From birth, all Elvar were taught the secret slipways of their mountain home, and as children played hide-and-seek in the slimmest crevices that led to and fro in the catacombs of their back yard. Before long, she heard the fiends' voices on the other side of the shaft and parallel. The caverns echoed beyond:

"Did we salvage no lamp?" one man asked.

"No oil," another stated matter-of-factly.

"We'll be bumpin' through the black all the way to the other side," the third complained.

"Trust me," the last consoled, "there will be light. Don't forget what brought us here in the first place."

Evendir's worry rose in measure to anxious concern – what *had* brought them here? Was this no accident, after all? It seemed the Elvar's secrets were leaked, and these brutes burgeoned with ill intent on their minds.

One bellowed, "Look! Writin' on the rocks."

Evendir stopped and felt the wall. It permeated with the souls of the long dead. They'd reached the Fool's Passage, in which recounted lessons inscribed into the rocks beneath the water's surface with the glowing inks of legend; the Elvar would read each and every one before finally breaking through the cove to daylight. Of course, these pirates were doing it all backwards.

The trespassers could not be allowed to live, but she could not take them on the boat with the little she had; she must wait until they were ashore again. Unfortunately, depending on the shore, shore would be too late – their edict forbade the Elvar violence upon others, even these interlopers, if they crossed into the Sanctuary's Heart. Only one path led that way, and there was no finding it without foreknowledge. Once they were lost in the catacombs and took to the shore along the skirts to find their way out, she would attack. Evendir exited her slipway and stepped out onto a bridge of stones laid by her ancestors, centuries before. This was the Graven Gap, leading the Shaft of Fortitude to the Shaft of Solace. The encroaching company passed under her without notice of their skulking predator.

"Where are they, Marryk?" a fat one spoke, bald and bulging.

"I don't know, Kreel." Marryk held a large harpoon in his hands, and was thick and stout as any Bayman.

The third sported a thick red beard down to his belt, "Maybe we're too late. Maybe someone else killed 'em all."

The fourth was no more than a boy in comparison to the others, but appeared to be their leader in the way they turned and addressed him when he spoke, "We don't really know how existent these myths of a people are, now. I've never seen one fer meself. 'Ave you? If they still rule these mountains, what are they – a race? A tribe? One family? All we know fer certain are the questions cloudin' the answer we expect."

The rugged swab appeared intelligent, or in the least astute, but appearances were surely deceiving here. The Baymen spoke, built and warred; however, thinking was truly beyond them from where the Elvar stood. And the Elvar were many. Just not here. The Sanctuary of Light was a sacred foundry where the Elvar coming-of-age journeyed to and through its dark as a rite of passage. When they breached the end, and looked out upon the Silent Sea, their journey was complete. Evendir happened to be on her retreat this moonscycle, and it was lucky she was.

From the Graven Gap, the pirates never once took a wrong turn, traversing leagues of waterways with precision. Where forks, splits, and drops in the subterranean riverland would have thrown even a creature of moderate intelligence off, these Baymen followed the true course. Was there a map? She'd never heard of one; even the scholars refused to sketch the designs of their natural home for fear of revealing it to the outside world. Each Elvar knew it by a shared oral tradition and common child-play misadventures. But a map would solve the other mystery as well; these brigands were not surprised when they saw the words illuminating from beneath the water's surface, the alchemically mixed ink upon the submerged legends and lessons. They knew where they were going from the start, which was a problem – fascinating, yet terrifying.

The company floated beneath the Arches of Aegis, the final threshold that led the band through a low culvert to where her own journey began. It was also the boundary, a border to the Elvar halls, which meant she could do them no harm the moment they passed under it.

Evendir cut through another slipway and found herself with the Gray Stair to her left, and the entrance to the Sanctuary's Heart at her right. The stair led back to the halls of her, and so many other's, clans; whereas, the *Rikdûmn* was what the intruders sought, and she heard their voices exclaim in wonder as they reached the culvert's dead end. It was a small room that brought the tides in to coalesce at a ridgeline that rose from a basin that drained the water's course beneath the mountains and beyond.

"Holy tides!"

"Blimey!"

"For *'zhri's* sake…"

Evendir entered from the Gray Stair's threshold and slunk back to the wall of the *Rhikdûmn*. Her cloak made her all but invisible to them. Elvar robes were sewn of silk that took similar color as the shifting shapes of the schist lining the Sanctuary's walls, and the entire culture were masters at Shadowed observation in stride.

The man named Kreel lost his breathe, his voice, and a few tears to the glittering landscape in front of them. The others stared agape. The *Rhikdûmn* was a cul-de-sac of shimmering rock, a ridge that rose from the waters in a blue-green schist that metamorphosed into an igneous array of iridescent stone. The walls themselves were a solid conglomeration of riches, gems, and minerals of a hundred different hues and qualities. It was a phenomenon, but the Elvar didn't question it. There was an altar at the cul-de-sac's vertex, which rose nearly six feet in height, to meet the breast of an Elvar on the short side, and it was emblazoned with a language these dumbfounded creatures would never understand and jewels they were all but obligated to steal: star sapphires mined from the seas without.

Their dinghy scarred the ridgeline and was left there adrift as the members of the shipwreck jumped ashore. The boy-captain held out his hand, "Hold!" Everyone halted their steps, but their eyes were on anything and everything else glittering around them. "'Ave we entered their treasury or their temple? This is either a place'a wealth or worship. If it's the second, we should take care."

The boy was right; they shouldn't touch a thing.

"Steal, but do it nicely," the bearded one affirmed.

"Right," Marryk agreed.

Sacrilege, Evendir thought.

The captain stepped up to the altar and felt its top. He brushed over what Evendir knew to be their Hallowed Tome, something unmoved for centuries, and pulled the consecration of so many down to study it. "Marryk?"

Marryk joined him. "Blank. Ya think?"

"Aye, mate." The captain motioned to Kreel, "Cup me some water."

Kreel removed a pewter cup from their pack, dipped it into the course's end, and handed it to his captain. The boy dumped it over the book and waited. They knew how Elvar texts worked, invisible until the tears of the *Evar'tûm* shed upon them; however, not all of it was so easy. "Nothing," the captain was disappointed.

"Who cares, Cap'n?" the hairy one cried out, "We're kings!"

Ignorance.

"Maybe," the boy replied warily. He alone gazed about the cul-de-sac as the rest of the pirates plucked the stones that hadn't been touched since The Five carved the sky. Focused ere his greed, he finally noticed the shape of the walls, how their faces shifted as the light refracted off the waters and hit them at different angles. "We're not alone," he spat frantically, stepping back.

The bearded one dropped to the floor, dead. Evendir spotted the insertion, where a blade bit the back of his neck. Someone else was here; she wasn't alone, and everyone, save for their captain, jumped.

"Who's thar?" Marryk called.

"I don't see no one!" Kreel bolstered.

"Calm yerselves, mates," the captain soothed.

"Razor's dead!" this was the fat one again, amusingly flustered.

"You are blind. As most of your kind," the voice was Elvar, but deep, male. She had an ally here caught in the same situation as her. However, killing anyone in this place of sacred reflection was wrong, no matter the cause. The Elvar revealed himself on the opposite side of the cul-de-sac, a step behind Kreel. Kreel spun to attack, but the Elvar turned with him and snapped his neck.

"Cap'n?!" Marryk called in question, oblivious as to what to do.

"Steady, Marryk," the captain ordered.

Marryk stepped back toward Evendir, who waited in the Shadows, nearly breathing down the man's neck, unseen.

The boy held up his hand, "We're trespassers here – I see that now."

"Indeed, you are," the second Elvar said.

"But, now we see ya. And now, it's two to one."

"Do you think me alone, pirate?"

He knew Evendir was there. Or he was bluffing.

The captain wasn't taking the chance, "Listen ... Lord of Stars, we were shipwrecked outside yer wondrous mountains, and there was no path 'round or through 'em. We were forced beneath them fer survival. We came upon this treasury and thought it abandoned long ago. We don't wish to harm or take anythin' that isn't ours."

"That is not what I heard, pirate," he spat back.

"Alas!" the boy cried, "Pirates. Pirates, to a fault, I fear. Yer people are a legend t'us; we honestly didn't even think ya existed."

"I see. You wish us to lead you out, then?" the Elvar questioned, a mock smile pursing his lips.

"Alive, preferably."

"Unfortunately, this is not a place for outsiders. How many others will come looking for these ... treasures, as you say, after you have gone and told your tale?"

"We may be pirates, but a Bayman's word's 'is honor."

Evendir noticed the captain was closer to her brethren now, his arms spread to show no ill intent, but it was there behind his storm-ridden eyes. This conversation was a distraction.

"We are a private people, and we care not for your petty Bight," her counterpart continued.

The captain reached within arm's length of him, and Evendir grew wary. This boy had tricks, she knew it. She spoke low and to the side, but didn't move, her voice echoing across the room in a way that no outsider could tell whence it'd issued. "Stop this. Our edict, brother."

The boy stayed focused, though a spark of curiosity leapt into his eyes.

"Is abandon here," her kin replied.

"This is exactly what it's for. We do not kill our lessers in this place."

In the distraction, the boy kicked his heel against the stone floor, and a short blade popped up, spring-loaded, from his boot into his grasp. He dropped to his knee, rolled sideways, and swept a slice across the Elvar's right heel's tendon. His enemy dropped to the floor in a cry of anguish: "Kill them!"

Evendir immediately shifted out of Shadow. Marryk brought his harpoon up to defend, but Evendir's swiftness was outright impossible to block. Her knife found his spine – she pierced into a point that paralyzed him on impact from the neck down. There was motion on the other side of the room, but when she finally had the chance to look, Evendir saw her other half disarmed and the boy's blade at his throat.

Marryk, hapless, leaned against Evendir and swallowed, "Cap'n. I can't feel m'legs. Everythin's goin' out."

"He's been paralyzed, boy," Evendir explained.

"So, what now? You kill him, and I kill this guy?" the captain replied.

"So, it seems." She wouldn't kill Marryk, not here, so Evendir pushed the man headfirst into the waters. As he could not swim through his paralysis, he began to sink.

Without hesitation, the captain threw his foe away and dove into the waters. The other Elvar scrambled back as best he could to prop himself up against the nearest wall. When the boy resurfaced with his mate in his arms, Evendir was at her brethren's side. She checked his wound and wrapped it; he would walk again eventually, but with a limp and a crook forevermore.

"They cannot be trusted," he quipped venomously.

"We don't harm our lessers, brother," she denied him. "We pity them. We show them the light." Evendir turned to readdress her enemy. "You saved your man's life, though there won't be anything to it, now. Why?"

"I don't leave m'living behind. Dead men rest, livin' ones can still dream."

Evendir thought on this, "What is your name, boy?"

"Captain Kaird of the *Bighter's Wrath*," he said proudly.

"You are not so evil, I think."

"You are," he replied succinctly.

This Kaird was hard, his loyalty steadfast. It would now be tested. "Perhaps we were both wrong," she said plainly.

"What 'appens now?" he asked, ignoring her remorse.

Evendir contemplated her options. She could forsake their edict, and kill them both, or she could teach him, show him Aegis through her eyes. "Will you follow me?"

Kaird pondered long on this. "Aye. I'll carry my burden. You carry yours."

Evendir nodded, and each helped their kind rise. While she could help her kin limp to the stairs, the captain was forced to carry his mate's entirety in his arms or across his shoulders. Evendir knew if the boy could make it up to the Evarseer like that, he deserved any revelations found there.

The enemies walked together up the Gray Stair, spiraling, carved out from the mountain's entrails. Miles of glittering stone steps and cragged halls of decorative patterns brought them to the exterior of a grand slope. They stood on a shoulder where a lichen-infested ligneous bridge led across a divide to the next peak. A light rain pattered the planks as the sky darkened. As they crossed, Evendir's ears trained on the conversation behind her:

"Ya need to leave me, Cap'n," Marryk pled.
"I'm not leavin' ya."

"Ya heard the daemon. What's m'life to me, now?"

"I'll find a way to help you," Kaird insisted, "I promise." He called out then above the winds, "What is yer name, Elvar?"

"Evendir Ûrotyr, of the Ko," she shouted back.

"Ko is yer clan, then?"

"Yes. And you are of the Baymen. But, not so stupid as most, it seems."

The captain laughed, "Yes, we leave our stupid back at harbor. Ya see us as yer lesser, but why? 'Cause, we live 'neath yer elevation? 'Cause, yer taller?"

"Because, we are better."

Kaird left it at that. The boy didn't care to argue. The rain never let up, and they camped the night under a short overpass of boulders protecting them from the rising weather. Evendir struck a fire, and saw Kaird drop his companion to the ground, suddenly weary. He sat, caught his breathe, then drew them close to the flames. She knew this would be a long, untrusting night.

Kaird motioned to her Elvar brethren, "What's his name?"

"Ryrenkûr Ûrotûm, of the Ka," he replied for himself.

"Sounds fancy."

"You ... are ignorant."

"I ... am funny," Kaird mocked Ryrenkûr's tone.

Evendir placed her hand on Ryrenkûr to stop him from taking the bait; she wouldn't let this Bayman play games with them. Instead, she traced her finger along her neckline in thought, a habit of most Elvar women. "You seem very relaxed for a captain who just lost his crew. His ship. His all."

The boy smiled, "My cap'n, the one who came afore me, was a good, bed-breakin' man. But, the fire-guzzlin' part of 'im was careless. Took us where we needn't go. Fooled us to sail when we should'a retired. We followed him, 'cause we believed. Then, I took up the cause, 'cause somethin' drew me in, and again, I believed."

"In a prize? A treasure?" Evendir was genuinely curious.

"Actually, fer most of us, it was you. We believed in you, yer secrets. We just wanted to know. Though a bit o' togs along the way would'a been nice. Ya can see that most of us paid the price fer it. I appear t'ave deferred my payment. Now, I'm just waitin' for the Shadow to collect."

Evendir nodded, "We need sleep. Shall I worry about waking on the morrow?"

"I give ya my word as a Bayman, I'll sleep as well as thee. Will ya take that?"

Evendir nodded, "I will."

They slept through the night and woke to the sunrise, a clear morning as ever she'd seen. Evendir rose first, Ryrenkûr second. The pirates woke late, but Kaird immediately lifted his mate and they continued on their way. Nothing, but the sound of the mountain, was heard through the morning and into mid-day. The storm clouds of evening came again, but were this time unthreatening. When the twin moons of Aegis were high in the star-strewn sky, Evendir stopped the company at an outpost guarded by three Elvar soldiers atop a watchtower. One dropped from his perch and met the company where the road cut a path beneath the holdfast. "What happened? Do you bring us prisoners, sister?"

"Not at all." Evendir helped Ryrenkûr into the arms of the soldier, "There was a misunderstanding."

"You have travelled far with wounded," the soldier eyed Kaird warily.

Evendir tread carefully, "They were shipwrecked near the western bays. Our retreat completed, I decided to take pity on them." Ryrenkûr was either too weak to argue, or decided by now to let her walk the path she chose without interfering.

The soldier lowered his voice, "This road is of single purpose. What is theirs with the *evarik*?" the soldier accused.

Evendir avoided the line of questioning, "May we take shelter with you? Dine and sleep within to ease our venture. We hasten our pace on the morrow."

"We will tend to our wounded brother, but you are unharmed, and we will not tend the enemy."

"Supplies." Evendir stated; it was all she could hope for, now.

"Very well," the soldier said at length. "We will not let you within, but will not leave you without."

Evendir nodded graciously. There was no faith in trust granted here, but what did she expect? The Elvar looked down on the Baymen with very little respect; in fact, they barely viewed them as civilized, though a civilization they were, spread farther than any other of the Realms as far as the Elvar scholars knew.

The soldier helped Ryrenkûr up the ridgeline and through the gates of the small, wooden outpost on the bluff, with its timber walls a perimeter hugging the mountainside looking out on the lands far below. The lee's crown had a clear shot to the north and south ends of the range, and was one of many markers leading Elvar in pilgrimages to the Evarseer.

When the fire was visibly stoked, a second soldier delivered them supplies without word, and they ate a small meal of stale bread and cheese. She was painfully aware how distasteful this was to her people, having Baymen on their peaks, let alone being led to a site as holy as the *evarik*. After Kaird had fed him, Marryk was the first to speak, "My Cap'n won't admit it, but he's gettin' tired. And I'm tired of bein' his burden. Where are we goin', and how far is it, Elvar?"

What am I to him? she wondered.

The boy-captain answered for her, "The *evarik*, if that soldier's accusation's founded. Our dear, late Captain Byrbor spoke of it often when I was 'is boy, as if it was an answer. 'Ask the *evarik* this. The *evarik*'ll tell ya that.' Is it one of yer kind, Elvar? Like an oracle."

Evendir pointed out where the end of the *Evar-aeor Ritûm* met the horizon. The range's final peak pierced the sky, taller than the rest, as if reaching for the stars. "It is a platform atop Mt. Evarseer. A place where the Elvar read the stars and talk to the gods."

Kaird scoffed without meaning to, then grew quiet, allowing the moment to pass. "Some of our people think *yer* gods."

Evendir smiled, "Good." There were many things the Elvar did to keep their culture clouded in mystery, to seed the doubts and wonders of man with the idea of the Elvar as deities. It protected them.

Kaird sighed and leaned back against a great fir tree, "Ne'er believed it m'self. And now I see yer a peoples like any other. 'Cept fer those long necks."

Evendir knew it was no insult. The two species who lived so very near regarding geographical distance, were incredibly different as it were in mind and body. The Baymen were a fighting people; contrariwise, the Elvar were reflective. The Baymen were short and stocky with thin red sprouts of hair, while the Elvar were tall, lean, with thick locks of onyx that flowed far past their lower half. The fact that their necks projected a whole lateral foot in height didn't help their delusion of aristocracy – they literally looked down on anyone they encountered. She'd never liked it, but the nobles took advantage of it. "If we rest tonight, but walk through the morrow's, we may reach our destination by the second dawn."

"I'm up fer it if you are," the boy replied. "Though yer burden's lessened of late."

"They will not take yours."

"I wouldn't ask 'em to. I'll get Marryk back where he belongs." Kaird resigned himself at this, and turned in. The night kept clear, and the three slept well.

The next morning, she found Kaird awake before her. The boy was strong, especially for his age, and his burden's stature – twice his own size in girth. They travelled, but did not speak, surely by exhaustion alone. Adrenaline kept the Bayman going through the day, but he was falling behind. Well into the night, she slowed her pace to match his. Now, with the sun set, she saw his adrenaline fading, abandoning him to the memory of his dead. Their spirits drove him now, she thought; her Elvar secrets were all that set them off on their journey in the first place, and now the lack of riches made it all the more important to find something, anything he could take back with him, to show the families of the dead their passing won a cause for the Embers. However drained, they stopped only once – they reached a naturally winding stair of rocky dikes that rose step by step up to the Evarseer's summit.

"Here," Evendir offered the captain her flask of *vitlan*. "It will refresh your strength for the climb ahead."

He took it, and nodded kindly; however, he didn't drink. Instead, he put the screw top to

Marryk's lips, who welcomed the quaff. Kaird handed it back to her.

At first, she didn't take it – what was he trying to prove? His glare was hard with purpose so she succumbed, took a draught herself and put it away. They ascended the dikes one by one slowly.

As the dikes narrowed, Evendir and Kaird, Marryk in his arms, reached a tunnel where she halted her companions. "We have come in time. The mantle of Shadow's flood has lit the stars bright for us, and the storm clouds have receded. When we reach the *evarik*, I will read for you, and the bleeding flame will show you the light."

Kaird hoisted Marryk over his shoulders one last time and followed Evendir into the passage. It was long and dark, but it brought them to the opposite side of the mountain's face, where they emerged on a ledge that sprawled above the clouds now masking the lands below. The outcropping was large and smooth, a flat deck that took the shape of an oval off the mountain's paramount like a coin balancing on the edge of a stone. There was a pedestal similar to the podium in the Sanctuary's Heart, except this book held the many records, dreams, and visions brought to the hundreds of Elvar who'd read the stars in this sacred place. It kept maps and charts of their movements in the night sky, as well as the seasonal projections of different constellations.

Kaird stopped behind her, and she heard him rest Marryk against the outer wall of the tunnel. The captain's footsteps brought him to the records, but he didn't reach for them as he had in the Sanctuary. Instead, he waited respectfully.

Evendir's eyes turned skyward, but a thin layer of clouds had rolled in and hid them from view. "We are better than you," she said aloud, studying the twinkling sparks behind the roils. "In our texts, there is a call to endow wisdom upon our lessers, guide them with our readings if we can."

"Yer texts want others to think yer gods," he replied.

"As we are the closest to them, yes."

"Are ya though?" Kaird doubted.

"I have never questioned it. You will see." To impress this boy may be beyond her, but to give him understanding would come all too soon. When the thin layer of clouds finally broke, the stars shone brilliant pinpoints of light that struck the rock face in patterns of light and Shadow. Areas of the platform – the *evarik* - lit brighter than others, while some captured the flame and fed the shine through cracks in the surface. Evendir chanced a glance at Kaird, and found him as he should be – awestruck. She turned her gaze back, from the stars to the stone, "There is much I see here, Captain Kaird."

"Is that so?" he tried to hide his new-found wonder.

Evendir looked back to the sky, she calculated their position and measured it to the signs of their shimmer upon the *evarik.* "A war is coming," she tracked the lines through the cracks in the stone. "A war that will cast all the Realms into fire, see them fall all beneath Shadow."

"Lucky us," he shrugged.

"You will be on the wrong side," she warned.

This grabbed his attention, "How d'ya mean?"

"Your kind will suffer greatly." There was something wrong in her reading, but she couldn't place it.

"I'm done fightin'. Nothin' ya say can change that, Elvar."

"Then you should not return home. The greatest city of the Embers will fall first ... and last." She pondered this herself, and saw the constellation Nûmyri flicker to unusual life, then diminish behind a passing veil of mists. "Strange."

"How cryptic of you."

Evendir shot him a glower of displeasure, "You would not be so unkind if you saw what I saw.

Woeful songs of betrayal and discourse will be sung of your people's fate."

"Can ya teach me how to read 'em, then?"

"No. That is not for your kind."

No matter his moderate temper, this aggravated his naturally brutish blood, "Then what're we doin' here?"

The night sky purpled since their arrival on the *evarik*. The clouds about the mountain's summit were thinning noticeably, and Evendir knew the sight to behold. At length to test his patience, she answered him, "Dawn is near. You have not come to listen, I think, but to see. Come hither."

Kaird joined her at the edge of the deck.

It would take a single push now for Evendir to drop from the precipice to her death, but she pushed aside that vulnerability drawing her hesitance. It shackled her to a single idea: He was still her enemy. *Is he, though?* she wondered. She knelt to the stone floor and waited for him to follow.

After a moment of what appeared to be a dreadful fear of heights, he crouched beside her at the ledge, then asked, "What're we waitin' for?"

Evendir didn't respond – it was no time for talk, but reflection. Evendir silently prayed for Mimyr's blessing in her attempt to broaden this Bayman's sense of wonder beyond that of physical treasure and measureable wealth. Just when the pirate began to fidget, the first rays of the sun's stretch across the horizon impaled the clouds below them, breaking them in a shimmering rush of spirit that lit the sky with dawn's revelation.

She knew Captain Kaird was speechless, staring at the overwhelming beauty of it all, so she decided to clarify: "The bleeding flame, we call it," she said, "It burns a fire that washes away the Shadow and brings upon us a new world with each new day."

While Kaird was blinded at first, his eyes adjusted, and the Realms of Aegis were revealed to him from the Evarseer's heights in the brightest light of the morning sun. The sky was clear, and he could see from the *Evar-aeor Ritûm* all the way to Cascade's End, thousands of leagues away. The effect was unreal, and even the Elvar didn't know how it was possible. They knew the world was round, but something from this particular peak, gave them a sight beyond the ordinary. Dyn saw the fields of Templeton, its cathedrals' bells glinting little flickers that caught the sun's rays. He followed the sparkling River Well up the Spine of the World to its font nigh a great city – Myrhaven – atop a mountain whose heights appeared minuscule to their own. He saw a wood vaster than any he'd known could endure, wide and flourishing on the opposite side of the world. Even Evendir knew not its name. The captain saw many things he could not recognize in tall tale or history, so many places he could never even dream existed.

Evendir knew how small the man felt on the *evarik*, and knew he'd seek a closer look in new, grand adventures, to make a mark over each league of discovery as the Baymen corsairs strove to do from king to king. She watched him stare, letting the landscape sink into his memory.

With a start, he fled. When she turned, aghast at his sudden change of heart, she realized he only ran back to drag Marryk to the ledge. Even now, he did not forget his last, frail crewman. She heard the captain whisper, "Ya see this, mate. There's so much more fer us to do."

Evendir knew she'd succeeded. She led the boy to understanding.

Marryk couldn't look away either, but addressed the Elvar woman, "Yer not gods," he said carefully, "But, ya seem to have their eyes."

She smiled, "And you are not so stupid, after all."

She left them there awestruck, glory rising in the captain's chest. If the two Baymen were meant to survive the descent, they'd do it alone, and she hoped their adventures would be many. Before she could disappear into the tunnel that led her back home, Captain Kaird called back to her one last time:

"Which side'll you be on, friend?"

"There was only so much even I could read," she replied and disappeared. In truth, she was escaping him to escape her own fate. She knew what side they would take, and she had to warn the rest of her people what was to come.

Anthology I

A Reignman's River

Nûrian, Trader of Pelts

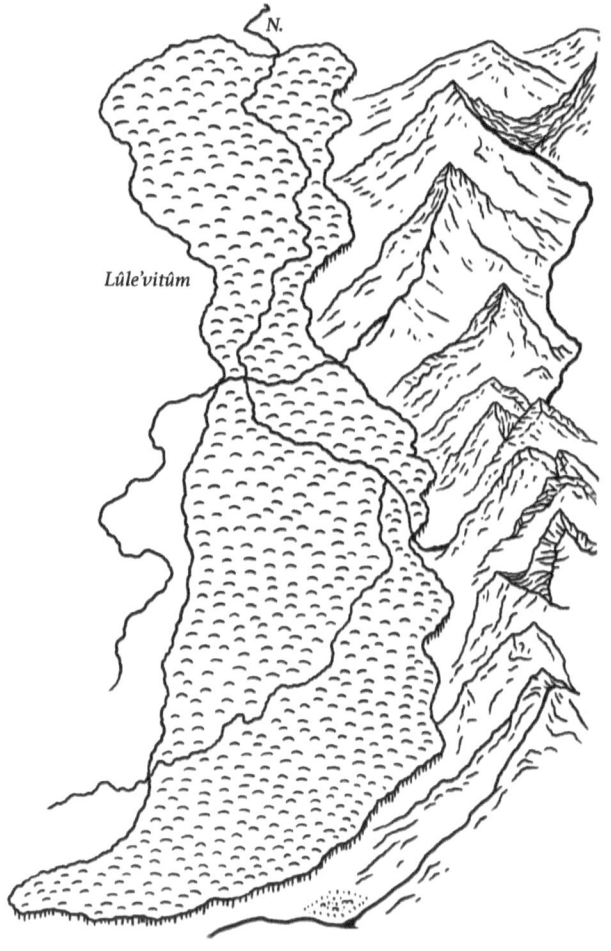

...being a short story during the Age of Origin,
approximately in the year 815...

With a forward stroke of his *pythe* – a long pole with a wide, incurved blade at one end to use in a sculling manner, and a thick mallet at the other used to push the scow away from dangers – Nûrian propelled the little wooden raft forward. He compensated with a backward rhythm only once, then drew the instrument of driving force from the water and popped it into its rest. The *Myr-hil* seized control of his lifeline, and Nûrian allowed the river to liberate the craft from mortal handle unto Aegis' escort. When the raft steadied, he released the *rhilar* – a balloon-like trap secured to the underbelly of the bow. It rumbled with the pressure of the surmounting undercurrent and caught a flux of eddies, launching the vessel as if it were an arrow through frothing clouds. It would carry the boat forward regardless of, and in many times in spite of, any undesirable winds. By luck or fatestream, for the courses were swift this morning, he prayed to Vyrlos, the Eighth, that he might see his daughter in a moons' phase's turn.

Nûmiel, six years of age with eyes that split the night, awaited him back in Damsford, a small fief just outside of Reignloch by the Silent Sea. A fortnight hence, he set sail in the hopes to sell or trade the many pelts he'd scored through the hunting cycles on his usual track east along the Reignway. However, ill luck befell him along that course – he sold very little, beaten in a timely manner by fisherman and hunters noticeably early this season. Upon reaching the Reignway's end, where it pooled at the Tears of Lys, he found even Templeton required very little, as they'd already stored out of caravans from the Barrows. He'd carried on up the Swanhelm toward the Spine, hoping that closer to the mountains, they would need pelts for the imminent snowfall in Dûntide – alas, little changed. When he reached Stonebarrow with ninety percent of his stock unsold and still aboard, the looming Shadow of the sparkling *Lûle'vitûm* dared his nerves. He refused to go home empty-handed, so he turned north, into this ancient wood – its stories old and powerful.

Nûrian, accustomed to the course and flow of the Reignway, found the *Myr-hil's* current strange. It swelled in an off tide, the ebb and flow changing by the hour, and crosscurrents cut random patterns from bank to bank by no logical cause and effect. When the river punched through a deceitful rise and descended into a natural valley, he discovered Islör. The little village sat in a grove where the valley had been cleared of its trees half a mile in each direction. Its people were kind, but superstitious of the woods. They had little to say, but housed him for the night and bought every pelt aboard. Contrary to their surroundings, which surely entertained more game than all the fields of the Reignhearth, the village bore few hunters, and animal skins and furs were in high demand. The people harbored quite the treasury of rare stones and minerals that Nûrian angled to sell on his return home; the jewels would go quickly, and the profit could last him and his daughter through Ilaeon. In addition to the bag of fortune's favor, he also nabbed a block of cheese and a case of fairwine – this for the road, or river ahead of him. The wine tempted him now, but he decided to save it for a celebratory dinner upon his breach of the weirding wood. If he could reach Stonebarrow by emberfall—

Nûrian's thoughts were interrupted by a high-pitched caw. He scanned the shores on either side of him, but saw nothing of real interest. The *Myr-hil* was on the slimmer side of waterways, yet he'd found its turbulence strove to feel otherwise, a younger brother of a greater man needing to prove his worth in short stature with great strength. His traditional rivers, that of the Reignway and its tributaries, were quite the opposite – broad and gentle. So were their surroundings. The Reignhearth, like its waters, was broad and flat. There were glades and kens here and there that sprouted up along the Realm, but it wasn't known for its woodland; whereas, the *Lûle'vitûm* was radiant, and late in the Withering Season mantled in a myriad of colors, shades of yellow and orange and red, no two leaves quite the same hue. There seemed to be a constant dew on their tips that sparkled in the sunlight. He could do little to understand the *Lûle'vitûm's* fare, but he appreciated the dense beauty of it all. It was all-in-all like none other for its majesty, albeit the eeriness of its legend, the devils that were rumored to reside in its canopies. Granted, all Nûrian saw on his trip north was untamed overgrowth, oddly quiet, but peaceful. Surely, there was more animal and insect life than the echoes of the *maccar*, but it was possible there were other streams teeming with activity in the woodland about him he just couldn't hear or see. After all, this one's violence was a ceaseless cacophony of tidal civil wars.

The shores tightened, and the embankments grew close and rockier, endangering the floorboards of the raft. If the waters grew too shallow, he feared beaching. He consequently used the *pythe's* blunt end to guide the raft to the river's center, hoping its heart's depth would not alter. Ahead of him, the canopy reached over the river's expanse in a dark knot of crooked limbs and tangled vines. The stretch of an eastern oak wove through branches of a western maple on the opposite bank. He saw them tremble, leaves rustling, but there was no breeze. His nerves heightened to attention. The rumors of devils in this shimmering wood came to mind, but the bedtime stories shared with the children of the 'Hearth to keep little ones from wandering were ridiculous. Then again, the people of Islör were afraid of something, afraid enough to rip out the roots of an entire dell to stay the canopy's influence on their homes.

Opening a bottle of the fair to calm his nerves seemed like his best bet, good for his hand and better for his spirit – it had been a long journey to the village, and it would be a long voyage home. A nerve-racked rafter was known to fall overboard at the first bump of the tide. Popping the cork, he took a whiff of its aroma – fruity, as was the fragrance of most fairwines. When he took a sip, his tongue caught a hint of warm lysberry, not in season this time of year, thus a nice respite from the cold.

He moved to the bow of the raft and eyed the canopy as it passed over him. For a moment, he thought he saw a creature bound from one branch to the next, but in focusing, the moment passed, and it was gone. The river swept him away, and all he saw in his wake was branch and twig, the colors and textures of bark in the brush. Unless the legends of the *Lûle'vitûm* were living twigs ready to snatch him up and chop him to bits for fertilizer, it was nothing. He thought very little on it afterward, taking a seat and laying back, humming a tune:

> *"I'd like a careful drift,*
> *Gentle on the way;*
> *I need a current swift and subtle tide to sing me home.*
> *I'd like a sailor's wind,*
> *Gentle on the sway;*
> *I need assurant whift and subtle guide to lead me home."*

As the river widened again, Nûrian sat up and saw the split. He knew from his travel north that the divergences would merge again at the end of a gradual incline, but only after the twins wrapped around a small isle that was home to a small grove. He'd taken advantage of it on his way up, to rest the night and deduce his bearings, but would have to pass it by now to achieve better time. Regardless, it was calming to know where he was. He caught the riverbed with the piercing end of the *pythe* and guided himself to the western fork. He'd sailed the eastern flank the day before, and was now curious to explore its twin passage.

It wasn't long before he found the two rivers differed – dreadfully so. The natural incline, which should have had him descend nicely on his return, was instead a shear drop in elevation that took him to rapids unexpected and deadly. Rounding a bend, the raft scored a large, jagged boulder that rose at the river's center, knocking his little boat sideways. He used his own stumbling weight to catch the blunt end of the *pythe* into the shallowing bedrock and drive his bow back south before the shift turned the whole vessel about. Straightening her out, he glanced back at his cargo – the crate kept tightly fastened – and his hand darted down to his belt – his little cache was secure.

A whistling shot past his ear, as if an arrow in close quarters. The sail caught it, a pinprick of a hole that frayed the flax. Strangely, a second whizzed by at a different angle, bank to bank, and it cut the sail lengthways. Its queer assault was cut short by the mast. The thing snapped and fell to the boards below. Nûrian picked it up immediately and found it to be a thin strand, much akin to wire, but nigh invisible to the naked eye. The mast's thick timber snapped it in two, and Nûrian thanked the Eighth for giving him a shipwright's blood.

The rapids worsened and washed over the raft. One large wave crashed into the bottles, but didn't have the force to take the wine and intoxicate the depths. Another slammed into Nûrian, who caught himself on the mast. His blood was a bosun's, but he was not his father; he knew this, and that his raft couldn't endure much more of this. Another whistling cut through the air, but this time considerably lower and ahead of him. It caught Nûrian across the shins, ripping through cotton and gashing flesh. He cried out and fell to his knees. "Hey! Who's there?!" He didn't expect an answer, but received one – a laughter on the western shore in the trees. Like children it was, light-hearted, but on its trail a maniacal cackle, a giggling of misanthropic intent. "Who's there?!" he repeated, but knew who it was – the devils. His heart sank.

The raft passed the isle, merging again with the eastern fork of the *Myr-hil.* Its pace quickened as thunder rolled, and he knew at this pace it would take him no longer than the night to reach Stonebarrow and the Swanhelm. It didn't seem likely these creatures would follow him past their own borders into the civilized world.

"How far does your reach extend?" he whispered thoughtfully; it was the only question that mattered now.

Dusk fell without further incident, which instilled a greater fear in Nûrian than if it were otherwise. Hours passed as the storm grew in measure, a torrent of rising current and vicious wind. He furled in the *rhilar*, the undercurrent's cross too rough on the thin leather. Luckily, he could keep the sail wide open; the gales blew south and increased his speed, as if the sky was assisting his flight to escape the clutches of whatever evil was lurking in the wood. The *evari* shone behind green-gray clouds, and somehow found its way through the storm-riddled black to burnish the waters, a ghostly mantle drawn over a shimmering grave. It caught movement beneath the tide, and Nûrian took a half step back instinctively, ready for the worst. As the raft came upon the ripple, it was a log. Indeed, it was a log before it sprang to life and limb. Its color, texture, and smell was a living extension of the *Lûle'vitûm*, and it seized the vessel's aft upon passing. Piercing yellow eyes shot through Nûrian's heart as the face of nature's devil stared into his soul from the end of his lifeline. The water flowed over the boards, but there was not enough force behind the creature to flip the laden boat.

Nûrian thought the thing mad if it were trying; then, he felt the shock from the bow and realized his mistake.

The moment passed like a dream, a breath caught through slackening mists. The tilt of the ship had raised the bow – it struck an incoming crag at the perfect angle, and the floorboards cracked clean through. The raft fractured between Nûrian's feet, as he spun to meet the catastrophe. He reached out to save his cargo, but slipped, as the vessel sheared in two and could no longer carry his weight. In his slide, Nûrian managed to plant his boot heel between the devil's eyes before plunging into the watery tomb.

The turbulence yanked him under, and the current swept him away. He felt the pressure of the downwash immediately, as the crosscurrents' battle beneath the surface was greater than the squall's wrath above it. Nûrian didn't have time to think on his lungs, crushing under the compression – the rocks came next. Sharp and rutted, he slammed into them. With his wits for the time intact, he shot out his hand, and by the Eighth's blessings managed to nab one of the boulders. Using the strength borne upon him by adrenaline, he pulled his head above the rushing water.

Gasping unto the living, he forced his breaths slow and steady. A calm head might grant him the chance to see his daughter again. There was a series of salient stones before him, as a road of massive pebbles crossing a pond. He wedged his foot against the rock he held and launched himself to the next in line, reaching out for dear life. From crag to slab, he propelled himself through death's fingers until he caught one wide and flat. He pulled himself atop it and kept sprawled, face down, to avoid sliding off. At least he was out of the water for a time, and he saw the shore only a few more boulders away.

Additionally, and abnormally, there was a large quantity of driftwood caught against the embankment; it seemed to line the path of stone like a lichen-infested reef. Another rafter had perished here recently, as he hadn't seen it on his way up; he swore silently not to share their fate. Unfortunately, there was no way to tell if any of it was hiding more of these malevolent animals, or a pack. He was unsure how they travelled, but he'd heard more than one voice echoing from the woods yonder. Only in his wildest dreams may they be more than ruthless spawn of twisted nature, but if they were, a plea for pity might save him now. He knew he had to try.

Nûrian carefully stood on the slab that held him and called out: "If you're out there, the ... peoples of this wood, I didn't mean to cause you alarm! Please! I'm only trying to return home; I have a daughter! I have a daughter!" He checked the bag at his belt – the gems were still secure. Even if he survived, if he lost those, he wouldn't have enough to keep his daughter clothed and fed through the season's cold.

When there was no response, he hoped for the best; he leapt from the shelf to the nearest pocket of driftwood. As soon as his legs hit the water, the rapids tried to drag him off and under, but he held fast. He pulled his way through the wrecks, the tide rising from waist to chest to neck as he fought. A broken mast's distance to the shore, the piece of hull he clutched was ripped out from under him – purposefully. Sinking in the force of the river's wash, Nûrian thought he caught a glimpse of the attacker, blood between its eyes where he'd landed his boot heel earlier, but his thoughts drowned in the fear of never surfacing again. He had nothing to hold on to, nothing to pull himself up, and the weight of the current kept him down.

In his despair, a second pair of yellow eyes snapped open before him, deep and hollow in a skull twisted and warped as an oak gnarled by the very tempest that raged beyond the river now. It was a different face, no wound from his frenzied punt. *They must travel in pairs*, he thought.

Regardless, he knew it was his end, and he thought back to his daughter; who would take care of her now? His love bolstered his strength and drove his survival. When the creature reached for him, Nûrian resisted, swatting it away. A second assault resulted in a tug-of-war between the two adversaries, descending, bobbing, and floundering. However, when Nûrian's back hit the riverbed, and the devil overshadowed him, his lungs depleted what little oxygen they had left in store, and his muscles gave in. The creature's fingers, long and spindly snatched him by the throat, as if trying to refuse Nûrian's body any involuntary breath that would result in drowning. Nûrian's eyes burned, and he felt his consciousness fading. Why wouldn't the devil let him die? He saw the devil's feet, toes sharp with talons like a *dûnvorr*, dig into the sediment below them. At once, they sprung upward, driving through the rapids even faster than they'd sunk.

Through spasms and coughing fits, Nûrian came-to when his arms reactively wrapped around a large piece of passing hull broken free from the driftwood reef. It wasn't for another few minutes, but he noticed his savior joined him. They floated in the rush downriver on the scrap together. "What – what are you?" Nûrian asked, teeth chattering as his body exhausted all its adrenaline, and finally felt the waters as they were – freezing.

The devil stared at him inquisitively. The flecks of color in its eyes twinkled, as a rising dawn broke through the storm and cleared the skies. It was thinking; it was intelligent.

Nûrian was unsure of all that transpired, now, "Are you helping me?"

It blinked translucent and vertical eyelids, much akin to a reptile's, twice, then rose his hand from the waters. It held Nûrian's bag of little treasures. "How old is your daughter?" it asked.

That was it, Nûrian thought – the devil, or at least this one, had a heart. "Six," Nûrian replied immediately, but continued warily, "She's all I have." He knew not if the creature was giving the bag back, or using it as leverage.

"Why have you come?" it asked, genuinely, wondering why Nûrian would enter a place haunted by such rumors as its existence proved true.

"I found no trade this year on the Reignway – the river of my home. My usual course. I couldn't go home empty-handed. We wouldn't make it through the Dûntide. What's left inside that bag is what will keep us both alive."

"This is our wood."

"I know. I mean ... I do now. I didn't before. Please, I didn't mean any harm."

"They like to play games." The creature stared past Nûrian to the woods.

"What?"

"My kin. We are the children of the Fourth. Sapling-born to curiosity. Sometimes our games go too far. I know this."

"What do I do?" Nûrian thought they were both doomed now if they didn't reach the border soon; it couldn't be too far away, he thought.

"Nothing." They reached another crag, and the devil used his legs to propel them against the dwindling current to the eastern shore.

Nûrian dragged himself into the grass and silently gave thanks to the Eighth before turning back to his savior, "Nothing?"

"They will follow me, now," it explained.

"But, why? They were after me..."

"They were after fun. You are no longer fun. I am a branch of the tree, now broken from the trunk. I am a traitor. That is more interesting than you." Its head perked up, listening. And then, it was gone. The devil disappeared into the shimmering brush of the *Lûle'vitûm*, but it left the bag of precious stones behind.

Nûrian's eyes traced back across the waters. He saw the canopy move, disturbed by whatever force of nature ultimately was after him the night before. He watched a dozen more of the creatures leap from the trees, diving into the river to cross its breadth in chase. He grabbed the bag and whispered blessings to his absent comrade, "Good luck, friend. May the Eighth bestow upon you angelic wings." In the end, it was the oddest course he'd ever sailed, and Nûrian wasted no more time – he raced south, by foot, back home.

An Eleaos'i's Abandon

Lökaeal'i, Master Toymaker

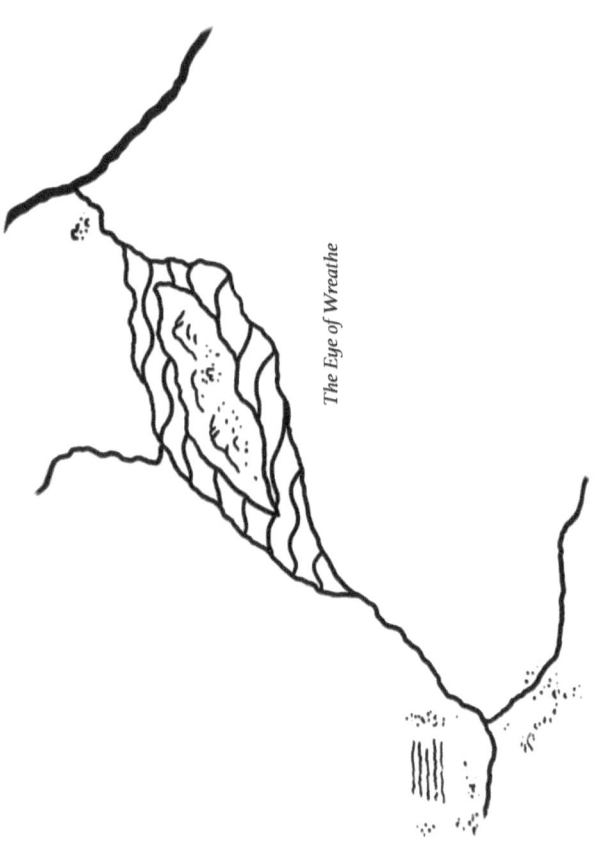

The Eye of Wreathe

...being a short story during the Age of Origin, approximately in the year 815...

Lökaeal'i stared at the battered Reignman, whom he'd pulled from the river's rapid clutches and saved from his kin's violent amusement just moments before. The doom this grace of pity wrought closed in on the Eleaos'i, engulfing him with terrible fear, and drowning him in a heartbeat that fell harder with each pound. Sympathy led him astray, and it may have marked his end; he shouldn't have done it, and now he took the Reignman's place as their target – a subject of ridicule, rejection, or worse. The southeastern banks of the *Myr-hil* lay just beyond the reach of his brothers and sisters ... for now, but they would move. They would press the Fourth-given boundaries of their gods-granted land. Their games would sadistically turn over, and warp with their displeasure. A patriarchal distaste for his betrayal would consume them; conscience was unheard of in what all Eleaos'i considered innocent diversion, what they called clean sport. Root-folk blood ran through his veins, and of kindred spirit he drew faith, but of mind – Lök saw things differently now.

Lökaeal'i ran before the stranger could thank him. With a fresh head start on his adversary, the Reignman would find his way home without impair, and the daughter he so verily pled for on the river's peril would need not suffer the loss of her father. Besides, by now, Lök's brothers and sisters had probably already forgotten about the simpleton, for they could care less about things that no longer amused them. This man was nameless; whereas, Lökaeal'i's treason no Eleaos'i had ever enacted or witnessed in the history of the Elm-born. They would pursue with a rekindled energy to play. In fact, as Lökaeal'i fled, he was mortified to hear just how quickly they caught up to his trail. By ear, he heard their bare, sharply taloned feet, spring through the crotches of trees behind him, while his own fumbled across the forest floor. By the hollow bone structure that braided around his temple, he caught the vibration of branch and twig as they leapt across the shimmering canopy of ash to cedar, elm to birch on an obsessive desire to see him punished. He flew to escape in a fleeting charge into self-exile. It was castigation or fratricide, but he would not turn and fight his own kind. That was unforgiveable.

When Lökaeal'i broke past the treeline of the *Lûle'vitûm*, he didn't stop, he didn't pause, and he refused to look back; instead, he climbed. Immediately before him rose the Spine of the World, the mountain range that spanned from the northernmost regions of charted Aegis to its southernmost expeditions. It separated the east from the west, and there would be no quarter in the west for Lök. Even if he could find a way to Stonebarrow or Templeton, they would never admit one of his kind – they'd all heard the stories. No, a promising future was not an accepting fatestream, he knew this, but it was possible, there were rumors, of a place in the east. Therefore, he climbed.

His pursuing kin would never follow him up the mountains – they could naturally bound through woodland, as it was their birthright gifted by the sacred elm so long ago, but stone was far from their ally. Lökaeal'i heard a cry of anger shriek from the trees, followed by a cacophony of tantrums as if all the children of the *vitûm* snapped in an intemperate storm. He clamored haphazardly up the nearest cliff face, his claws scratching and slipping every inch of the way. By a miracle, he reached a ledge that rose a league higher than the farthest groping limbs of the canopy. He stopped.

He breathed. He addressed his home with great regret – there was no turning back now.

Sixty days and sixty nights passed in uneasy mornings of wayward anxiety and evenings tormented by Noxukûr, who brought him the faces of his brothers and sisters cackling in madness and raving of his villainous betrayal to commit an act of compassion on one of their victims they so enthusiastically considered volunteers. After all, each one willingly entered their wood, knowing what dangers lurked in the Shadow. However, luck was on his side in physical travel; the regular cycles of snow had yet to fall, and he welcomed a revitalizing rain. Moreover, with his diminutive stature and natural kinship with the wild by his side, Lökaeal'i found it guileless to avoid the many harmful beasts and short-tempered mountain clans by taking the nooks and crannies few others could slither through. The pockets of glades and fen brought solace as he kept to their canopies. However, when he dropped from their heights to the foothills of the Spine's eastern rim, the question that haunted his rebellious passage rose in measure, once whispered, now a chorus of doubt and cold introversion: *Where to go?*

He surmised no civilization of sensibility or pride would take him, but knew he could not live alone for the rest of his days; his kind were not nomads. He recalled the first rumination that made its way through his hopeful flight from the *vitûm*: In all the caravans that passed through their wood, there was but one place everyone spoke highly of, a fortitude in acceptance, like a distant dream or lover, welcoming and warm. It was a longshot – if it existed at all – but, he had to try.

Before him lay a wide stretch of yellow grass, blades thin and gently caressed by the breeze, as far as his eyes could stray. All there was to do was keep walking.

The days ran long and uncounted, as there was no change in elevation or growth for leagues. The miles seemed immeasurable. The sun beat down on him mercilessly during his waking hours with no shade or tree, small or large, no oasis or riverbed as far as he could find. Nightmares continued to stalk his sleeping; some ended with his limbs in chains hanging from the split elm of their birth, while others ended in a pyre of his own bones burning him alive. Each outcome held one thing in common – the eyes of his kin judging, glaring in disapproval, hanging the hemp or holding the torch themselves. It was relentless. He prayed to the gods to grant him grace, kindness, even pity if it would alleviate their cruel delight in watching him suffer;

however, his prayers fell on deaf or callous ears, unanswered through two moonscycles.

Lökaeal'i collapsed at the banks of a mirage, or so he thought. When he found the flow swift and sure and shimmering as the wood he'd left behind, he leapt into its current abundant with joy. He waded to the center of the South Wreathe River, and stood motionless for a time.

At length, he looked about him: To the north lay a tightly packed conflux of towns well industrialized, but to the south the river's length continued on and faded over the horizon. Farther east, a small farm house with expansive tracts of wheat and barley spanned with pastures of fat, healthy cattle. There was a barn a good distance out from the house facing south, large enough to house a stable and more. He entertained the thought of stealing whatever horse resided there, but he had no desire to enter the city of understanding as a criminal. Nevertheless, he was weary and beyond exhaustion, so he took that road east and crept into the barn through its second story window, out of sight and out of mind, even to himself. He could hear voices above the occasional whinny of a steed and bleat of goats. This farm was well-off and run by a boisterous fellow:

"Did ya hear about Rowland?" he guffawed. "Poor lad was caught in Old Man Cantor's place."

"Again?" a second, rougher voice responded, "Courtin' Erys again, eh?"

"I wouldn't say courtin' so much, though he got himself good use of those dancin' feet when they were caught. Leapt straight out the window, right through the glass and sprinted to the next quarter. Took to a chapel for sanctuary."

"No..."

"Yep."

The farmers shuffled about and Lökaeal'i could hear them brushing and feeding the faunae in turn.

"I swear," the second continued, "if that girl ain't wed by plantin' season, Mistleton'll burn by the blue moons for all the lads denied her. Dûnkrath be tame vie a woman scorn."

"And lonely," the owner added.

"*Aera*. Worse at that."

"How's yer flock been, Tinder?"

"Last night, lost three," Tinder sighed as he filled the water troughs.

The owner's fist slammed a stable gate shut, "What?! Trail or track of what did it?"

"Nothin'. Couldn't tell ya if it were man or beast what killin' 'em. But, if it keeps up, I'll lose it all," Tinder sounded despondent, as if this account was an everyday occurrence.

"Shame. You'll end up broke at the gates of Nûmundor."

"Wouldn't dare. Strange place, that. Ya know, I heard the Thrush-King…"

The conversation continued out of earshot as both men took leave of the stable, their nightly chores complete. Lökaeal'i peered over the loft's sill to find quite the menagerie of farm stock. A great black stallion stood in one corner where stables erected a private quadrant for him, while half a dozen goats were penned in its twin. A gaggle or two of *lansid* were fenced at the center, while a sty of pigs snored in harmony in their own private box. A cage held three birds of unknown origin to Lök; however, he surmised they were used for conveyance between here and this Mistleton, most likely the conflux he'd seen north of the river. Their dull colors and short feathers defined them far from birds of visual pleasure or show. Lökaeal'i sat back in the loft and rested his head on a pile of hay.

Thoughts of the great Nûmundor relaxed him, welcomed him to sleep. For the first time since his escape of the *Lule'vitûm*, he did not dream of his cackling kin, and Somnyr pulled him into a far more deepening slumber than he desired.

He did not wake to the sounds of morning; instead, it was a boot heel in the ribs that ripped him from his rest. "Hey! What in the name of Vyrlos are you?!" the farmer shouted at full volume, snap-brim hat shading his eyes and a pitchfork's prongs threatening Lök's jugular.

Lökaeal'i stammered incoherently, as no words formed through his dread. He shoved himself back frantically until he met the barn wall. The farmer followed him, "What manner of devil – *aera!* You must be the thing what's been on Tinder's flock at night!"

Lökaeal'i didn't have time to respond or confidence enough to plead for better; the farmer bore down on him madly. The Eleaos'i rolled away from his thrust and sprang over its shaft. Out of the corner, he leapt over the loft's edge, planted one foot on the stall nearest his path of descent, and bounded from horse – whinnying with discontent, but receiving a whispered, "Sorry," from Lök – to pen to entrance floor. He filched a cloak from a hook at the threshold of the barn and fled. He could have easily killed the farmer, but desired even less to enter Nûmundor a murderer than a thief, such as he was now.

Large and billowing, the cloak almost tripped Lökaeal'i on multiple occasions as he raced from the tract and sprinted east. He never took the time to look back; if the master of the farm wanted him dead, he could surely mount up and ride Lök down – granted, the equine in the barn may have just been used for plowing, far from battle-trained. Lökaeal'i's surge from peaceful rest to escape and survive quickly drained as the morning fell away and the sun beat down again. He longed for the woodland, the effervescent shimmer the sun wove through those thick canopies. It would bounce from one dewdrop to the next in cascades of little watery treasures. Surrounding him now was nothing but plains and tallgrass. They had a simple beauty of their own, certainly, but it was nothing like the *vitûm*. Amber and citrine were the colors of harvest, of the fleeting moments before the end of natural life through Aegis' womb; contrariwise, his lush place of birth was viridian and alive! It was a land where many of the trees didn't even lose their color in winter's tide, a fight for life and growth against the bleak and piercing cold.

As dusk fell and the first glimpse of the moons peaked in the east, Lökaeal'i came to the River Wreathyr – as the signpost named it. There was a small port at river's end, at which ran ferries between the heart of the Wreatheland and the Vesper Shores. Whatever men inhabited this place, they were surely no different than the farmer. Whatever ill weather, nocturnal attack or bad luck befell any one of these poor people would all too easily find blame through his mysterious presence and strange ugliness. Lök pulled the stolen cloak about him, hiding what features he could, but he could not hide his feet, his crooking talons, emerging from the trim with every step. He was a beast leaving wild footprints in the ground as proof to fear his passing.

Lökaeal'i kept to the Shadows well enough through the faintly lit streets, no more than dirt paths heavier trodden than the surrounding soil. When he reached the ferry and saw a passenger drop a few copper coins to the harbormaster's desk, he realized what he should've much earlier – this was civilization, and he had nothing to barter but the stolen cloak on his back. In his despair, the clouds cleared and starlight shone brightly across the river, which revealed two things: First, Lök could see the ring of trees that marked Nûmundor's glistening rise over the horizon beyond the Eye of Wreathe's isle of hillocks upon the Wreathyr; second, the harbormaster saw by moonslight his face, now illuminated beneath his cowl.

"Demon!" the man cried. Everyone around Lök spun to meet the man's accusation.

Lökaeal'i didn't bother to react further; without hesitation, he jumped the chained barrier to the river and dove into the rapids. While they were a cool respite from the heat, he could hear the shouts from the shore rising behind him. He swam east, downriver, as fast as he could manage, and did not tread water or attempt any rest until he reached the Eye. The shores were rocky, and he slipped and fumbled up to a short plateau by climbing exposed roots reaching for the river. When he pulled himself over the edge, he dropped to hands and knees in overabundant relief. He felt the grass between his fingers – it was green and verdant – and dug his talons into the soil he considered freedom. "Thank you, mother Aegis, for allowing me this respite, for granting me guidance and sanctuary."

The great Nûmundor will accept me, he thought.

The stares of the Nûmunyr were no different. His visage was as devilish to them as the harbormaster, the farmer, the Reignman. His skin the texture and color of soft bark, his appendages long and sinewy as twigs, his very walk a stalking predator with the piercing gaze of a bird of prey – they saw him as a disfigurement of nature, that which bore Nûmundor its grandeur by godly design. He'd come so far to find a greater distance in their eyes than that of the Stretch he'd crossed. The eleven trees that rose as the ringed wall, the very structure of Nûmundor, were as a new prison, mystical in their ascension toward the storm threatening the yard. They branched like eleven brothers locked arm in arm defending the city as one, and their limbs were so fashioned that guards of the watch patrolled their catwalks without fear of falling. When he passed through the open gates, a portcullis jagged by nature, but hard as stone and sharpened as steel, trimmed and cultivated to deathly precision at its eleven speared ends, Lökaeal'i found the city itself was laid out in the same perfectly symmetrical ringed approach. The market was set against the outer ring upon entrance, but fletcher's stations resided on either side of the eastern gate to supply the wall on necessity. The inner ring held homesteads erected against either side of smaller *estras*, a version of oak that grew wider than its cousin and largely hollow. Platforms were built through the *estras'* interlacing canopies acting as balconies and play space for children or romance. A natural river was redirected by man to embody a third ring, a perimeter for a magnificently vibrant court; it entered from the Eastern Gate, flowed through the city and exited at the Western. The northern and southernmost trees of the outer ring held star-hewn receptacles, basins at their heights that fed rainwater to the river ring by wondrously constructed waterfalls. They had already started their flow as the clouds overhead produced its gift to them.

Lökaeal'i wandered through the market, then turned down an alley to reach the inner ring. When he reached the river ring and its courtyard, he found the heart of Nûmundor. The stronghold palace of fashioned timber was a twelfth tree the Nûmunyr carved and bored into a kingly hall so glorious Aegis herself could not cry for their use of her, the many blades that pierced her to sculpt it. After all they'd done to it, the massive boon still grew, still flourished and flowered in acceptance of their hand upon Her. As he stared at the marvel, a child fleeing the rising storm bumped into him, knocking his cowl from its barrier to his face.

"Oh, I'm sorry, I –" Lök started, but the child screamed and ran back to whom appeared her mother, burying her face in the many golden folds and sapphire layers she wore.

"It's all right, dear," she comforted the girl.

"Is it a monster?" the little thing peered back at Lökaeal'i warily.

"Well, I don't know, sweetheart," the woman answered, unflinching at neither Lök's appearance nor the rain falling harder by the minute. He knew he was a poor sight for such a beauty as she, deep auburn hair and chestnut eyes, compared to the shining knights and strongmen inhabiting the rest of this great city. If she saw him as anything more than insignificant, he didn't presume; it was verily possible she simply had a courage others did not as to visually withstand the grotesque and weird. "Are you a monster?" she asked him.

Lök opened his mouth to reply, but couldn't, didn't know what to say even if he thought he deserved to say anything at all to someone of such grace in this harsh world. Instead, he allowed fear and doubt to best him, and he slunk back into the alley from whence he came. He watched from the Shadows as the woman ushered her little girl indoors. No one had ever spoken to him with such plain attentiveness before. Did she not see his ugliness?

When he turned back into the market, the streets were muddied, and most of the townsfolk had retreated indoors. As many of the shops had a well-maintained overhang, they didn't so much close as simply withdraw to their rears or backrooms to wait out the shower. Lökaeal'i presumed it to be a daily occurrence. His attention was caught by a little shop wedged between a fletcher's station and a garment house. Nigh unnoticeable in the bustle of morning shopping, it was apparent now in the empty streets. A boy bounded out of it aglow, a smile spread from ear to ear, a wooden knight in his hand already defending against invisible foes. His father exited right behind and guided them home.

Lök stepped up to a cloudy window no larger than a burrow. He peered through and saw other carvings and toys of similar design. He pressed his face against the glass to try to make out more of the cheerful wonders of a child's world within.

"Ahem," a throat cleared astride him, startling Lök. A man with a bushy brown beard and bright clear eyes stared at him from the threshold of the toy shop. "If you'd care to clean m'window, use a rag instead'a yer face." He tossed a rag from his belt, and Lök caught it deftly. If he was disturbed by the Eleaos'i's appearance, he didn't show it. "Yer good with the hands. And yer ugly."

Maybe not, Lök thought, and drooped his head, "I can ... I can whittle pretty well, sir."

"Sir?!" the man bellowed. "Let me tell ya somethin', son, whatever ya are: Whatever ya are ain't no longer what you were. If yer here, it means ya left somethin' behind. Leave it there. Who you were is gone. Yer a Nûmunyr now and forever, son, and we're all equals here, whether ya be you a beggar or Highest Lord of the Marches. Only one we call Sir here's the Thrush-King himself, and let me tell ya, he don't like it one bit either." The man's face wrinkled into a smile and laughed. "Ya say ya can carve, I believe it! And I may be able to find a place for ya here. Ya like kids?"

"I'll scare them away," Lök's stutter was gone, but his confidence still waned.

"I can't say we don't have our judgments; all man does, but every Nûmunyr's judgment is a natural reaction to what is." His voice dropped, "Look around ya, son." Lök hadn't realized the man had moved closer, but he draped his arm around the Eleaos'i's shoulders now, a good head taller than the Elm-born, "Look at what is."

Lök glanced up from the streets drowning in mud and rainfall to the shops and Shadows where men and women waited for the storm to pass. He hadn't noticed it before in all the glory that was Nûmundor, but many of them weren't as Lök first perceived. The blacksmith was burned from ear to navel on his left side, an accident most-like, leaving him scarred and disfigured. The baker was missing an arm, some injury of some distant battle leaving him lame in the eyes of most. An old, bald and disabled man sewing a dress in the back of his stand was in fact no man at all, but a woman! She whistled happily while she worked, blind but grateful and refined. Indeed, the many peoples of Nûmundor were probably all bullied out of whence they came, but drew together in this city of life, confident and accepted.

"We all got our demons, son, whether it be that which scars us on the outside or that which dwells within," the man continued. "Show 'em what ya are as a Nûmunyr, and they'll no longer see ya as anything else, but a friend." The man splashed back to his shop's door.

Lök removed his hood slowly and let the rain bathe over him, as if washing away all that he was before this moment. "I love the rain," he said without cause.

"Aye. We get a lotta that 'ere, not too far from the Vesper Shores and all. What direction you come?"

"The west."

"Across the Stretch? Sure is a long ways; let's get ya fatly fed and properly clothed, eh?"

The man led Lökaeal'i inside his new home.

Cycles passed, the moons carrying the seasons on without much change until harvest came upon them. The anticipation of festival spread the laughter of children about the city as they begged their sires for just one more toy from the marvelously odd toymaker. Lökaeal'i had doubled his master's production in no time and experienced the joy he once felt so long ago with each smile on each child's face his hands had a hand in. He'd whittled more knights than could have possibly consisted the King's Thrushmen, though he heard a battalion was making ready for some holy crusade soon, which upped his sales. Lökaeal'i found the Thrush-King odd in his own right as well; very few had ever seen the man, save those closest to him, and he was heard to venture from the palace only when the moons were high and the night was clear. Some claimed they'd see his silhouette walk the ramparts of the brothers during the strongest storms, but that rumor was mongered by those citizens who wanted to see him closer to a god than a man. Lök had never seen the man himself; in fact, Lök rarely saw anyone that didn't come into the shop. He spent so many hours happily at work, that his spare time was expended climbing the brothers' arms and bounding away through the nearest canopy, all the while the guards watching and cheering him on. An Eleaos'i's skill was far from common knowledge here, and Lök enjoyed showing off. The Thrushmen quickly became his close friends, and even those without scions would come visit him in the shop to see what new wonders he'd crafted that week. He was finally accepted and looked fondly on. He thought he was happy.

Then, as the Ûroghas festivals neared with the coming of winter, with the city preparing for the year's first snowfall, she came back into his life, the mother he'd met his first morning in Nûmundor. It was after his master had retired to his bedchamber that she came; she entered the shop in all the elegance he remembered, as if her daughter had ran into him that morning. Tonight, she was in a cotton olive as the leaves of the deepest elms of the *Lûle'vitûm*. A laurel of flower petals adorned her temple, as was common custom during times of festival and harvest. She chuckled at the sight of him, "I heard it was you. The man causing so many children to smile, so many sires the loss of their hard-earned coin."

Lök's face tilted down; he couldn't help but stare at the floor. This may be his home now, but she was well above and beyond his reach. He never desired love for himself in the cycles he'd lived as a Nûmunyr; he never found it necessary, and a small part of him feared rejection because his kind, still so different in nature and physical appearance to the rest, was more beast than man. "Some of them, ma'am," he was at least able to stir up the confidence to converse with her this time.

"You never answered my question," she continued.

"My lady?" Lök didn't understand.

"Are you a monster? Have you come to steal the children you beguile away in the night?"

"No, ma'am," Lök almost smiled. Almost. "No monster. I am a simple Nûmunyr."

"Good that you finally figured that out," she stepped up to the counter.

"Can I – can I help you with anything, ma'am."

"My name is Asira, and first you can step from the Shadow."

Lök didn't move.

Realizing his insecurity was not one to provoke if she wanted friendly acquiescence, she continued at length, "I'm looking for something special. For my niece."

"Your niece?" Lök perked up at this a little too noticeably.

"Yes," Asira nodded, "You've met before, I believe."

"Aye. I remember." So, the little girl was not Asira's daughter after all, which meant she may have no children, may not be married at all. *Was it possible,* he thought to himself. *Did it matter,* the thought threatened.

"Well?" she prodded.

Lök snapped back from his daydream. He pointed out a shelf of dolls. "Well, we have a nice selection of—"

Asira interrupted him, "Normalcy, yes. I want for her after my own tastes – something different, something unique."

"Hmm." Lökaeal'i considered this, "I suppose I could custom carve anything you'd like if you have something in mind."

"Where are you from, toymaker?" she asked.

This surprised him; nobody else cared about his past – he was a Nûmunyr, they had no past farther than the moment they stepped through the Greengate. "Not a very nice place, ma'am."

"Was there nothing beautiful there?" she pressed.

"Oh, no, I – I mean, yes, yes," Lök's spirits rose, recalling his lost wood, "So many things." He stepped from the safety of his Shadows in excitement, using his taloned, three-fingered hands to help visualize his explanation via gestures of importance. "Shimmering things with silken wings; dazzling dewdrops at dawn dancing across the newest petals of the richest colors; magnificent beasts of nigh mosaic quality leading wild hunts across a land that itself pranced in growth by the Fourth's design and the Ildraeor's blessing."

"You miss it," Asira surmised with a sad smile.

"Only in the waning hours of twilight, for I recall all too often the musical notes of the midnight lark singing me to sleep that does no more. But ... I belong there no longer. And it does not compare to the beauty here."

"I will be the judge of that, I think," she challenged. "Make my niece one of these beautiful things."

Lök nodded, "Of course."

"How long?"

"A day," he answered immediately, surprised at his own urgency.

"Very well," she smiled a smile that warmed him through the long, sleepless night.

Lök took soft wood, string, fabric, and spring, everything he could find to construct what he'd never attempted – a memory, true and precise. He'd never reached so deep into his past since his self-exile, and at times it hurt, but at others inspired him, igniting the flames of passion that in turn fell in love with her. He allowed this feeling to fuel him; while he could never ask for her love in return, he could share his own for her through this work. With each groove, he rounded edge into elegance – his dance through the canopies – and with each incision he cut in floral design lay his caress. The outer item for this machination he hollowed and split down the middle, hinging it on one side. The inner piece he slipped inside, folding layer upon layer of silk on top of itself until it was neatly packed, its lacerated ends pinned to a release joint across the beauty's body. He painted the shell, the cocoon, plainly to warrant surprise within, and when the morning hues shed through the small window and washed over his workspace, he saw his masterpiece complete, waiting to be opened.

Before Lök could succumb to exhaustion, a knock came at the door. As no one had need for locks in Nûmundor, he simply called back, "Enter!" and stumbled his way through the debris of supplies he'd left cast aside during the night.

When he reached the storefront, he found a family of four browsing – he relaxed. Through hours of eternity in which this ordinary day passed, he waited on customers, each knock and every footstep, praying it would be her presented in the threshold, the toy hid deep in his surcoat's pocket. He'd advised the master to take the day off, but didn't elude to why. Regardless, the man was glad to do so with the intent of seeing the newest show put up on the Thrushfeather Stage – another grand retelling of Nûmundor's birth.

As the sun set and Lök's eyes could no longer keep alight, she came to call; however, she was not alone. Asira wore a deep crimson version of cotton she'd worn the day before, but the man next to her wore the chainmail and pins of a lieutenant in the King's Thrushmen. She presented him, "This is my brother, Lieutenant Galaborne. It's for his daughter you worked through the night, master toymaker."

Lök bowed his head in respect, "It's an honor to serve the Thrushmen."

"It's my daughter you're serving," Galaborne laughed, "and she's hard to please, trust me."

"Children fancy action and mystery. Beyond all else – the unknown."

"Sounds more like my sister here. Let's see it, then?"

Lök pulled the shell of wood from his pocket.

"A cocoon?" Galaborne asked.

"Aye. A cocoon," Lök smiled, prepared for the displeasure in his tone, as it would soon turn into wondrous impress. "But, look! This cocoon holds a secret inside." Lök pressed a groove at the shell's bottom. The hinge sprang open and a creature with silk wings glittering in the candlelight dropped, hung suspended by strings secured to the cocoon's mechanisms.

Galaborne was pleasantly surprised, "A butterfly as a marionette – thoughtful."

Lök shook his head, "Not a butterfly, friend. This is a flutterspark, a creature of magnificent depth that keeps to the darkest groves of my home where the canopies of the wood black out the sun entirely. Watch."

He had Galaborne's attention, but more importantly, he had Asira's. Lök pressed the hinge's barrel sideways and two strings were drawn up, letting drop their lacerated folds – "Fire!"

"*Aera!*" Galaborne cried out with a laugh, shocked at the brilliance. The new folds glistened with gold and were laced with crushed sapphire that refracted light all about the room.

"A flutterspark," Lök explained, "can willingly ignite itself. On its own volition. Either to scare off a predator or to attract a mate. Some claim they've used them for lamps, but I find that cruel. The rest of the spark is resistant to its own flame, and the secondary wings here grow back once exhausted."

"Things are not only not what they appear," Asira studied, "but have great depths in which they can be reborn again and again."

"Aye, ma'am. You asked for unique – there is no other place on all of Aegis in which the flutterspark can be found. The *Lûle'vitûm*, the land whence I hailed before calling myself a Nûmunyr, is the only place."

"It's impressive," Galaborne stated. "You outdid yourself, I think."

"I love my work."

Galaborne nodded, "I'll take the doll over there, the one with the curls and frills and blue eyes."

"I'm sorry?" Lök didn't understand.

Galaborne picked up the doll, "What you made last night, you did not make for my daughter. Though I'm unsure that was ever the commission's true intent." He eyed Asira, then dropped a piece of silver on the counter with a gentle smile, "I believe she'll love it."

Lök wasn't sure which product the man was paying for or which person his comment referred to, or even if the man was upset over it; nevertheless, the lieutenant left without another word, leaving Lökaeal'i and Asira alone.

"Is your work all you love?" she asked at length.

"It's all I have, ma'am."

"You've never wanted for more?"

"Not until last night, ma'am."

"My name is Asira. And he's right, I do love it. This flutterspark. I look forward to seeing the beauty in all you have to offer beyond your toymaking." With that, she took the re-encased flutterspark and glided out the door, whisking away with her his heart.

Anthology I

A Nûmunyr's Crusade

Galaermus Galaborne, Knight-Errant

The Stormstone Cascade

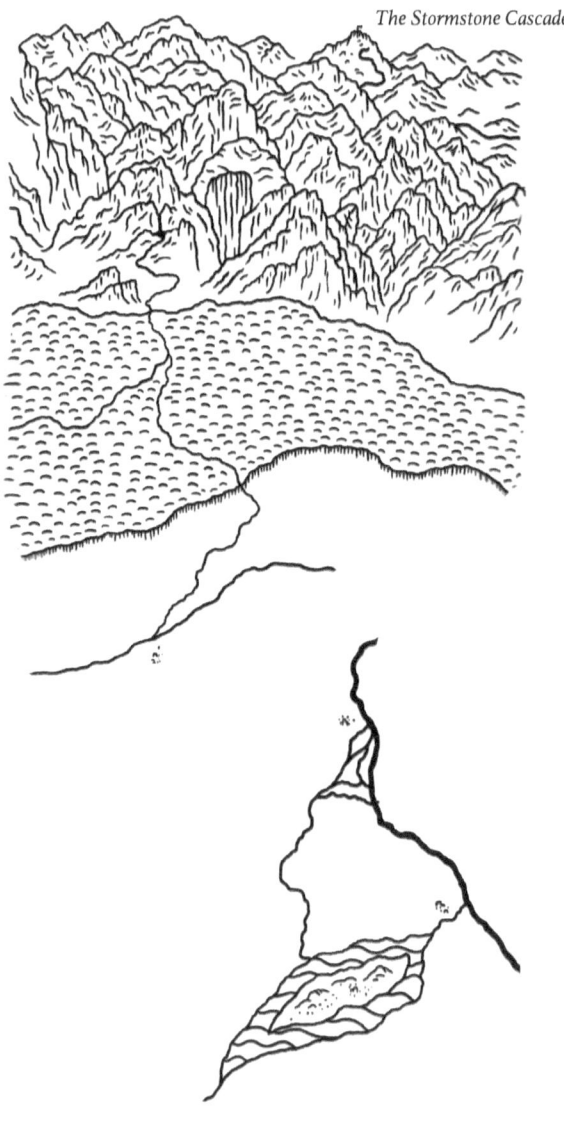

...being a short story during the Age of Origin,
approximately in the year 819...

With great purpose, Lieutenant Galaermus Galaborne's long strides brought him to the Whisperhall. Two fellow Thrushmen opened the great oaken barrier in silence, hinges oiled every six hours to keep the humble hush of peace; however, as he entered, Galaborne couldn't quiet the clank of the steel that fashioned his boots. His heavy footfalls on timber echoed through the still, fragranced air – it smelled of lavender and thyme, as did the rest of the Thrushbough Palace. The Whisperhall's vaulted ceiling and rounded walls revealed every word spoken there, for the hollow tree led every secret whisper to the King's ear. There was nothing hidden from him; and in turn, he hid nothing from his people. Rumors had already spread of a holy crusade, so Galaborne knew in part why he crossed the gilded expanse, floral designs glistening in shades of green and gold through the annual rings that wove through the floor's wooden panels. He couldn't help but feel in awe each of the few times he'd been called upon here. The palace itself was twice blessed: First,

Aegis allowed it built through one of her own unnaturally large and winding *estras*; second, by enriching the coffers of Nûmundor with the natural treasures used to adorn her laurels, priceless coats of gold laid by those that could only be gods-given artisans. When Galaborne reached the Thrush-King, he clasped his hands behind his back alongside his liege, mimicking the posture of his lord of power and vision. Then, he waited.

At length, Thane, the Thrush-King, raised his voice to a lonely susurration, audible only for the utter silence held over the reverent hall, "I've had a dream, Galaborne."

Galaermus kept his voice at the same finite decibel, "Sir?"

Thane spun on his heels, "I hate that," he whispered curtly. His face showed signs of unrest, his stubble left unshaven and his hair unkempt. To its contrast, his clothes were of the finest lavender silks, clean and trimmed with gold, sporting an olive lining. Its train trailed across the floor as he crossed the room, barefoot. He stopped at a bronze pedestal that rose and split and interwove, extending into a sculpted canopy suspended from a niche in the domed ceiling. The thin, twig-like shafts twined down and around each other like vines of a small metal jungle, and a half dozen thrushes perched among them.

One, speckled white, caught the King's eye, and it fluttered down to meet him at eye level. He stared at the little bird, "I built Nûmundor on a dream. Did you know that?"

Galaborne nodded, "A vision. Yes. Your people regale it often on the Thrushfeather. On that stage and off. Eleven trees you saw, boughs reaching like brothers-in-arms to the next – a ring of defense, strong and terrible. It guided you here, and you erected a city with the help of a single old man. A wizard some say."

"A wizard?" Thane smiled sadly, "Wizards are not real, captain."

"Never believed that part myself – wait," Galaborne paused, "Captain ... sir?"

"I hate that," Thane stroked the thrush's head, "Yes, captain. The lesser of two reasons I summoned you. But, first, you know I was just a boy when Aegis called my name in that story." He cocked his head back to Galaermus, "I am an old man now, and She's called it yet again."

"How can I help you," Galaborne stopped before he repeated the word sir. Thane saw the word as considering someone else less important just because of a chain of command, which he also despised, but knew was pertinent for civilization to run smoothly.

"You are the dream," he continued.

"What?!" Galaermus forgot his manners entirely, taking a few steps in surprise until the egregious sounds of his footwear snapped him back to where he was. The echoes of his voice faded, and the Whisperhall calmed him again.

Thane raised a finger, "However, there is much of the first dream the people of Nûmundor do not know. Whilst I do not keep it from them, none have bothered to prod further into myth and magic than its humble beginnings. Their hunger is satisfied with the little they regale."

"Tell me." Galaborne was enthralled; it was verily possible no one had spoken with the Thrush-King for this lengthy of a time in ... *well,* Galaborne thought, *ever.* Even the welfare of the city at council only heard a sentence here or admittance there of agreement or disapproval.

"A fire rained down on the walls," the King continued. "As eleven brothers, the *estras,* stood fast and mighty. But, a Shadow loomed on the horizon – chills my bones, even now – and when it came upon the city, it engulfed the brothers and drowned the people." Thane twitched, his ear perked, "What?"

"Sir?" Galaborne asked. He had said nothing.

Thane raised a hand to quiet the newly anointed captain. The King lowered his head to the thrush nearest him. "Yes, yes, I'm getting there," he assured the little spark of jitters. Galaermus thought, *could he truly talk to them, after all?* Thane turned around to address the knight directly, "there was a ... star, or something much akin to it that shone beneath my feet, beneath the very world when the sky was lost."

Thane crossed back to the large bay window carved from the side of the palace's trunk and treated with stained glass – it depicted a thrush at one end taking flight from a small branch, and followed its motion from panel to panel until it reached an identical twig at its counterpart. He looked out through a semi-clear panel to the plaza below, "It glowed. A beating heart in the deepest black. From this, rose the twelfth tree."

"A twelfth tree? The palace?"

"After we built it, I drove a hundred tunnels through a thousand meters of catacomb beneath our feet, mined every inch of Aegis' womb without compromising the very roots that kept us afloat. I found nothing, Galaborne. There was no Heartstone here."

"Could you have..." Galaermus dared to ask, "Misread the vision?"

"Ah. I thought so at first, too, as what does a boy know about such things anyway. But, no, a boy also simply knew nothing of patience."

"Now, you dreamt of me," Galaborne was starting to understand.

Thane looked at Galaborne, who saw a deep thought in his King's golden eyes flecked crimson, a trait he'd seen in none others. "I saw a man," he said at length, "Virtuous and pure. He rode a blood-red mare into battle, bearing the coat of arms of a true Nûmunyr. He was a soldier born to us, under us, a gallant herald to the Thrush."

Galaborne felt himself tremble, which unnerved him, "You say much of me, but know me little, sir."

"I know you better than you know yourself."

It took all of Galaborne's discipline not to step back at this, for there was power in his words. "The people ... some people ... say you can talk to the gods."

"Do they?"

"Can you?"

Thane looked back to the brass canopy and chuckled, which carried through the Whisperhall as if it were a haughty bolster from the stoutest Fyrzhor, "The ability to speak with a man speaks nothing for his divinity. Or omnipotence. I can talk to anyone I wish if they wish my council, or if I wish theirs. As such, I have spoken with your friends, your family. You are the man in my dream. I know this to be true, Galaborne."

Galaermus felt a twinge of fear pluck his heartstrings one by one as the tension in the Whisperhall drew across a now lingering reserve. He didn't want the responsibility of the very life of Nûmundor on his shoulders. That was for gods and kings, not a soldier.

Thane finally continued softly, "The roan fell to a mighty enemy. The coat of arms shattered into a thousand slivers. Aegis bled dry. I saw the rider reach out his hand." Thane's attention turned back to the window; the sun was sinking on a velvet horizon, "The Heartstone – it now wants to be found."

Nothing sounded clear to Galaborne, but Aegis did not whisper to him as it did the King.

Thane retreated from his station and collapsed in a small wooden chair in a set of common furnishings of no great value, humble in contrast to the elegance of the hall itself. The King hand-carved them himself to always remind him whence he came. Though, no one really knew where that was. Seated and withdrawn, the Thrush-King looked so small, not a King at all, but a man. Galaborne noticed a slight, uncontrollable twitch in the man's right hand; thinking on it now, no one even knew how old Thane was, or how many years Nûmundor had stood tall. There were few histories kept in the town, and only the King had an official chronicler. They just knew how it was, why it was, the myth, the legend, never a timeline. "Are you alright, m'lord?"

"Lightning flashed across my vision," the King ignored him, "the rider fell through the earth." With his steady hand, Thane poured himself a cup of wine, deep purple near black within the wooden grail receptacle. "Glistening, Galaborne, like the rays of dawn on crystal waters was where he fell, deep beneath the world, closer to the womb of Aegis than I think man is meant to walk." After finishing the first cup, he poured a second and motioned a come-hither with two fingers to the thrush, who flitted over and pecked up a few sips. "Long away and far ago, the Heartstone was forged where light meets Shadow beneath a White Hall."

Ignoring, or so he did his best to, the strange sight of the thrush intoxicating itself, the captain thought on the dream. "The lightning," he surmised, "was the Stormstone Cascade."

Thane nodded, "I believe so. Ride north at dawn. There must be a people hidden under the mountain Shadow who have secrets we need."

Galaborne nodded and made to leave, disquieted again by his clanking footsteps. The Thrush-King raised a hand when the thrush on his shoulder piqued his interest. Thane closed his eyes. "A warning Galaborne. Dreams do not come in a linear light. What I saw was a circle of hands as it were, some of it may be closer to the present, and much may lie far in the future. We cannot tell for certain."

Captain Galaermus Galaborne rode out from the eastern gate of Nûmundor blessed by the Winged Deacons and supplied by the best Thrushsmiths in the city. Across his back was strapped a great two-handed broadsword folded so light he could wield it with one. Over it lay a silver filigreed shield bearing the fleur-de-lis of the city – a crowned thrush with twelve rings against a golden sun. The bloodmare that carried him was given years ago by the Orsain Horselords for his sacrifice in the Second Barrens War. It was a steed with as many honors as he and, possibly, even greater deeds. Stormblood they called her, for she neither frightened by the flash of lightning, nor paced at tempest's squall; she welcomed the storm instead. Galaborne never had need to spur her or crack the reins; she kept her pace at the need of her rider without prompt and through all exhaustion. As the captain thought on his King's twitching hand, he knew haste was needed, and they drove across the Eye of Wreathe within an hour. They slowed only when they reached the north ferry, which would carry them across the Wreathyr to the banks of the

Wreatheland. Many Wreathelanders considered Nûmundor a part of their land, but the Nûmunyr did not. They were a separate entity of different beliefs and lifestyles and goodness.

Minutes later, his two compatriots caught him up and reared to a halt, "We'll need to follow the trail of you in no time, captain. A figure on the horizon, you'll be," Tristlen said in a huff, patting his stallion in thanks and readjusting the quivers of arrows bunked, one angled above the other, across his back.

"Stormblood will not lose you, have no fear of that, Tristlen."

"No, no," Lamorek, the third of their gallant company, shook his head, shifting his narrow shoulders to better support his own load of shafts, "He means he has no sense of direction in the first place – ask him for north."

"Which way is north?" Galaborne asked, a smile threatening his lips.

Tristlen kicked Lamorek in the shin, "I know where Lamorek's wife is right now. Does he?"

"That would be south," Galaborne added in jest. The archers had been his friends for as long as he could remember, and he trusted them with his life. He would need their eyes in the dark wood afore the Cascade. He would enjoy their company as well. There was no telling if this people under the mountain Shadow were friend or foe.

When the ferry dropped them off at the northern banks, they rode in silence across the green hills and pastures of the Wreatheland's plenty; the terrain was easy on their mounts, the ground soft and subtle in its changes. They stopped once at midday on a barrow that rose a watch above the rest. Rotting timbers told a tale of a farmhouse once in residence, but long since abandoned after whatever mishap burned it down. Stormblood and her lesser kin grazed, but no one slept, and they were all off again before the sun had noticeably shifted.

At day's end, Galaborne saw a fjord of many streams threading just a half day's journey ahead. When Tristlen and Lamorek caught up, he pointed out the obvious, "If we ride through the night, we could reach the fjord by tomorrow's evenfall."

"Somewhere along that tree line is the Gatestream," Tristlen offered. "We'll follow that path into the *Everö'vitûm*."

"What kind of folk dwell under those canopies?" Lamorek asked.

"We've explored a small minority of the wood, only enough to route a trade convoy. And we've seen none. As far as we know, there are no inhabitants," Galaborne explained.

"As far as we know," Lamorek felt the need to repeat.

"There's too much resource in that vast a wood for it to be empty of life," Tristlen mused.

"There's trees," Lamorek shrugged.

"We should be careful if its people take measures not to be seen by passing caravans," Galaborne warned.

The riders rode through the night, and on through the next day. They crossed the fjord as the sun set and the twin moons of Aegis rose bright in a cloudless sky on the second. It was a clear and shallow crossing, and their steeds welcomed the cool tidal caress on their hooves. The Gatestream branched off from the fjord's fingers and directed into the *Everö'vitûm* where a bowing cedar formed a natural threshold into the wood. Beyond it, pines grew dense and thicketed. Their horses slowed to a trot upon entrance and followed the trader's path for a time; however, as it wound east toward the Vesper Shores and the small fishing villages along the coast that was the Nyri Bay, the riders led their horses off the beaten soils of cart and journeyman, and turned into the thick, dark mass of overgrowth.

Tristlen and Lamorek unhooked their bows from their saddles and laid them across their legs casually. They were each fast enough to ready and draw at the slightest disturbance, "It's getting darker," Tristlen observed.

"The limbs are growing wider, reaching closer to their kin. The canopy is closing in on us," Lamorek's eyes shifted about nervously.

"Should we stop, captain? Our horses are tired. And there's not much for us in this dark."

"At the first break," Galaborne agreed. "I enjoy groping in the dark far less than your keen eyes give comfort."

When the light of the moons appeared again, they came to rest in a little grove beneath a star strewn sky. Compared to the pitch of the wood, it was as if dawn had already risen. They set a ring of stones and built a small fire.

"What if there are enemies afoot?" Lamorek asked.

"We're enemies to no one here. I shan't have us act like it. We keep the flame low, but if we attract attention, so be it. I would be glad to meet whatever people inhabit this mysterious place. For all we know, it could be prosperous for Nûmundor."

"Nûmundor?!" the harsh whisper was released in surprise from somewhere behind, yet all around them, as if the very trees gasped.

All three riders whirled around to immediate attention. "Tristlen?" Galaborne asked.

"I see nothing. Lamorek?"

"Nor I, captain," Lamorek replied in turn.

"But ... we are not alone," Galaborne settled.

"Interesting, how quick they were to spot us," Tristlen studied, "There must be many of them in a land of this size if their kind stretch from here to the mountain."

"They might not be one and the same. We are not yet under the mountain's Shadow."

Tristlen took the first watch, nervous as he was now. His fingers caressed the yew of his bow and plucked mindlessly at the fibrous string. Every wisp of wind that rustled the leaves, every creature of the night that crept by and retreated from their firelight, every stray thought of the unknown pressured the strain on his discipline. The cold, haunting air grew tight about him; his muscles stiffened. He paced to warm his blood, between Galaborne and Lamorek, both fast asleep. After growing tired of retracing step after step, he decided to patrol a few feet away from the camp's perimeter. Little could be seen beyond the small radius the moonslight reached, but Tristlen's eyes were keener than most. He scanned the deeply threaded canopies, expecting whatever may be watching them to dwell in the shelter of height, any forest-dwellers to be masters of tree. However, when his eyes came down from their ascended guard, the creature was there. It stood on the ground staring at Tristlen from a few yards out, half-hidden, but not in hiding, behind a large pine sheared on one side by some bolt of lightning long ago.

Alarmed, Tristlen jumped back, but kept his mouth shut. His heart raced and breaths quickened. The adrenaline pulsing through him now warmed his system and he was suddenly alert, ready for anything. By knightly honor alone, he kept himself from notching an arrow, for Galaborne was right, they did not want these people to see them as enemies in their own wood; instead, he raised a hand, "We seek that which Aegis whispers as Her command. We do not intend to trespass beyond borders not our own, and seek only understanding of the road we must follow to the mountain."

The creature didn't move; in fact, Tristlen was unsure if the thing was even breathing, let alone understanding him with any ability to communicate. Instead of proceeding, which was not the Nûmunyr way in such a situation, he took a step back patiently. He kept his eyes forward on the smoldered pine until it receded from sight. At this, he turned his back to it and returned quickly to the fire, knelt before Galaborne and shook him gently until he awoke, "Captain?"

"I thought it were Lamorek's turn," he spoke up groggily, "What's happened, then?"

"I saw it. It watches us," he replied.

Galaborne was on his feet before Tristlen finished. He gave a single kick to Lamorek, who jumped to the living with leaves caught in his mouth of egregious snoring. He spat them out and whispered curtly, "Are we surrounded? Did we surrender?"

Tristlen looked to Galaborne, who turned and questioned Lamorek, "...what?"

"What?" Lamorek stammered to his feet.

"Never mind, let's go." Galaborne doused the fire and the riders mounted up. While the horses were having a difficult time passing through the ever-roughening terrain, they did as they were bid until they reached the unique pine. It didn't take long.

"There," Tristlen pointed, "It was there."

"Do you think the horses spooked 'em?" Lamorek suggested.

"Possible. They surely have no need of such beasts here, but must have seen some leading caravans on the trade pass." Tristlen was certain everyone in all of Aegis knew what a horse was.

"If they wish to present to us, they will," Galaborne assured his comrades.

"What's the course, now, captain?" Tristlen asked.

"We present ourselves, I suppose. Find out if curiosity is enough to draw them out again." Galaborne raised his voice enough for it to carry, but not so to sound hostile, "To whomever finds interest in me and my friends, I am Captain Galaborne, Knight-Errant of Thane, Thrush-King of Nûmundor—"

There was a hiss from nowhere and everywhere at once again, but no more. Galaermus continued:

"And these are my loyal Thrushmen, Tristlen, exile-heir to Mistleton's Lordguard, and Lamorek, born of our great city and a Yewman strong. We seek only safe passage through this wood. If you claim it for your own, we seek only your permission to allow our journey forward unto the mountains. Upon our return from the Cascade's depths, we hope also your tolerance if not your blessing." He ended it there, and they waited in silence.

Lamorek fidgeted in his saddle, "Such a pretty speech if no one was there to hear it."

"You got to hear it," Galaborne smiled; a bit of levity was needed in situations of tension like this to ease men.

Tristlen focused, "No. They heard you. I see shapes moving in the Shadows."

"How many?" Galaborne's hand drifted nearer a position to draw the blade from its sheath at his back if the need arose.

"Half a dozen, maybe," Tristlen replied, though not confidently. "Wait ... the dark is still again."

"Did they stop? Or disappear?" Lamorek's voice betrayed his nerves.

"Settle," Galaborne said gently.

"I – I can't say," Tristlen shook his head. "If only I had Lök's eyes right now," he recalled the Eleaos'i who'd befriended them all leaping through the canopies of the Wreathe's Eye akin to a squirrel. What he wouldn't give to be tree-born now. "But, these people do not seem like they call this home. If they did, would they be watching us from the ground, apparent on the forest floor? Nay, they would just as easily be holed up in the canopy."

"Maybe they want to appear as unthreatening as we do," Galaborne pushed.

"Or are confident in their position to attack."

"Could be nomads. Do the Nithûr reach this far south?" Lamorek asked.

"I've seen one or two cross the city's path, but I wouldn't say as to their eastern and western direction, or the providence of such. They don't travel in packs, though," Galaborne deduced. "This can't be any Nithûr to our account as we know them."

"There!" Tristlen called. "Movement north, but by single, or possibly a pair alone. Do we follow, captain? They don't seem a hasty folk."

"Then whoever they are, they don't see us as a threat, after all." Galaborne thought for a long moment the consequences of tracking this intrigue. "We follow, but only as they walk north. If they veer, we do not; we carry on to the mountains."

Hours passed as the riders followed the Shadows north. When the rising sun broke through the myriad of needles flushing the sky, a soft orange glow illuminated the brush. Tristlen pulled back on his reins to draw his mount to a halt, "They're gone. I've lost them."

Galaborne nodded, "For now. You need the rest that Lamorek and I received last night. We'll keep an eye out, and break fast when you awake. We have time enough for that at least, I think. If they want us to catch up to them, we will when we're ready."

The dawn came and went, and Galaborne pressed Lamorek into further sleep without difficulty. While they rested, he studied the woodland, calm in its morning routine. He could hear a *lanser* flock fly somewhere overhead, and the mid-day songs of the blackfeather skylark soothed him. Galaermus had ventured many places for the King in his days – Mistleton on its river conflux and many stilts, Rötbale past the Wreathmire, even as far as the Ildûm'tyr, once a lesser part of an envoy to the power of Seerhold, in an attempt to barter a trade deal with Fyrnûr Bay. They had succeeded and many Thrushmen still wore that priceless armor now. Galaborne's shined brighter than ever to this day. Whatever creatures or peoples they had followed the previous night were far different than any Wreathelander, subtler than any Fyrzhor, and travelled too many to be Nithûr. These people were as ghosts in the moonlight as anything else; which in part seeded fear in Galaermus, but sparked interest the same. After all, the unknown never failed to fuel his adventurous side.

When his friends rose, Lamorek poached some eggs and Tristlen gathered greens. Galaborne cooked them with a few sausages brought from the city before mounting up again. As they traveled north, they met with a second stream, contrastingly wide and rapidly flowing with current and eddy. They kept to it, drank from it, bathed in it, and carried on. Their horses did the same. Most of the woodland critters were hidden from them, simply by natural evolution of coloring in the dense thickets; however, none in the company had spotted any sign of a predator for which even the smallest hare would fear. The birds were not carnivores, as they ate berries from a variety of bushes, and the largest hunter that crossed their path was a red-tailed squirrel chittering after his desired lover amidst the maze of trees.

Night fell, and almost immediately movement was afore them again, "They're back," Tristlen confirmed.

Lamorek jumped in his saddle, "Captain!"

Galaborne turned, ready for an attack; instead, he found idle eeriness. Tristlen pivoted silently with him and saw the reason for Lamorek's exclamation: Two of the creatures were now on either side of Galaborne, one between he and Lamorek, the other between he and Tristlen. They walked casually at the same steady pace as their steeds. They wore robes in colors of deep blue and cobalt. Clasping their cloaks were broaches of intertwined shapes, seven, silver-fashioned and subtle. When strands of moonlight breached the canopy, even Tristlen gasped: The faces of these people were so pale, they were practically translucent, as if they were indeed ghosts, but Galaermus could see the veins beneath their bald temples – they were without doubt flesh and blood. They had a thin form, but their legs must've grown long, because they stood a head taller than Galaborne's saddle, and Stormblood was already a greater size than most of her kin. "Friends," Galaborne directed his attention to both, though they did not pay him any heed in return, "Is there anything you could tell us of this wood? The maps brought to Nûmundor by trade tell us very little above its name – the … the *Everö'vitûm*?"

Before they could await an answer, a screeching howl split the night's calm into a symphony of nocturnal unrest. "*Scarborr!*" one of the strangers cried out and knelt, putting its ear to the ground, "*Aera!*"

"Captain?" both riders prodded in unison to their commander.

"Draw!" Galaborne ordered. "Form a ring around these two. If they need no protection, we'll soon find out."

"There!" Lamorek sang.

Galaborne turned just as Tristlen let an arrow fly. It struck the largest woodland beast Galaermus had ever seen. The steel-tipped shaft pierced the creature's flesh where he surmised its shoulder was hidden beneath layers upon layers of leathery muscle. The pig-like thing didn't sway; instead, it answered the attack by completing its own viscous assault. It tore into the hind legs of Lamorek's equine, which toppled over on impact, pinning its rider to the ground. When the beast addressed him, Lamorek swung his bow around – a crossbar against the pig's snapping maw. Its crooked canines gnarled through the yew, and it bore down on the knight.

Galaborne was out of the saddle when a second shaft whistled past his ear and struck the beast's jaw, turning its bite away from its prey. It looked up in time to find Galaermus' sword arcing in for the kill; in response, it bounded off Lamorek's steed with no more than a gash to its natural armor. "The flesh is too thick," Galaborne called out, "more steel-like than leather!"

"Aim for the eyes, archer," this came calmly from one of the strangers, who Galaborne saw now were still looking on, unmoving from the initial protection zone.

A third arrow found its mark in the beast's left eye. It roared in pain. Galaborne sidestepped to position himself on its right, then thrust his sword into its other. Without sight, it raged blindly and retreated back from whence it came.

"Do we pursue, captain?" Tristlen reared.

"Nay," Galaborne waved, moving to Lamorek's aid. Tristlen dismounted to help. Together, they hefted the fallen stallion away, and the man rose with a hand clenching his side.

"Ribs."

"Broken?"

"No, I think that beast would have made a fine rack of ribs."

Galaborne smiled, "Are you alright?"

"I think so; what were they doing?" Lamorek motioned to the strangers, and on closer inspection, all three riders saw the tips of sheathes trailing out the fringe of their cloaks – they had weapons, and did nothing.

Galaborne nodded Tristlen to see further to Lamorek, so as he could turn his own attention to the strangers, "You can communicate with us, but cannot fight by our side?" he asked.

"We do not kill the children of Aegis," one answered calmly.

"It was attacking us," Galaborne argued.

"It was attacking you," the second corrected.

Galaborne shook his head, "You don't think that monster would have come at you once we were safe in its belly?"

"No," the first stated matter-of-factly.

"If you don't fight them," Tristlen added from behind his captain, "Why the weapons? And how did you know where to aim?"

"Just because we do not make war on something, does not mean we do not know how to fight it, Nûmunyr."

Galaborne tread softly now at the discreet threat, "You know us, we've gathered this; would you allow us the same courtesy?"

The strangers eyed them and let an unnerving silence set over the night, the moonslight casting a ghostly glow beneath their hoods. Their eyes were lit with a starry luminosity, like blue sapphires floating in a foaming sea. They turned back north, one after the other. "Tell me, how far has Nûmundor come?" they began, leading the way.

Galaborne remounted and motioned for Tristlen to do the same – Lamorek would ride with him. "How do you mean?" Galaermus did not quite understand the question, as Stormblood trotted behind their procession.

"Who sits the wooden throne?" it rephrased.

Galaborne shook his head, "Nûmunyr has no throne."

"Is that so? Then, who leads you now?"

"Thane, our Thrush-King, the same as built our great city."

"And you think he has no throne?"

"No," Galaermus replied matter-of-factly.

"Interesting."

"Who sits yours?"

"The six of one and one of six and all."

"Is that a council, then?"

"Of sorts."

"What do you call yourselves? Your kind, your peoples?"

"The *Dirkas* keep the perimeter," one said at length. "We keep watch afore the *Evendöt*, and walk the lands the *dûmni* keep, but keep from."

"That sounds strange to me," Galaborne admitted.

"Much we say will sound strange to you Nûmunyr, and much we do you will find unnecessary; however, we take care to care for what we are and protect."

Galaermus read between the lines, "You know why we've come, then."

"We know why all seek the Shadowalkers. There is much Aegis gives us the Fyrzhor themselves can do little to recreate with their unholy forges. But, it is dangerous walking the Vein of her womb between light and Shadow."

"I will take your heed and bring with me caution, but we will find our Crusade won through any peril."

"It may not be peril that finds you, Thrushman."

Galaborne thought on this riddle a long while as the strangers led his company through a maze of paths invisible to them, directing the company through the dark as if there was some present road that none could see. Without these strangers, Galaborne knew they would have twisted and turned blindly through such woodland in their attempts at continuing north, and probably would've found themselves lost. The moonslight fell away beyond sight as the pines grew thicker, and it became harder to see the figures leading them onward; however, Stormblood had more than sight at her disposal to track these Moonsguard – *Dirkas*. She had their unique scent in her nostrils, now, and her hoof prints following their boot prints.

As the sun's rays inched up and began to bleed away the night, the company reached a small clearing. Once more, Galaborne saw they were abruptly alone. The strangers vanished as morning threatened with the breaking dawn.

"Where did they go, you think?" Tristlen asked no one in particular.

"If they were ever there at all," Lamorek mused.

"Does it matter? Whether by curse or blessing, they led us to where we needed to go," Galaborne gazed in awe at a gaping hole in the earth just before its rise in measure to the first hazardous steps of the Stormstone Cascade. They were indeed under the mountain's Shadow now.

The entrance to their objective was before them. A giant ash tree bowed over the chasm.

"The horses won't make that," Tristlen observed.

"Lamorek," Galaborne ordered, "You'll ride back with both our friends here, report to the King what we've found and let him know that Tristlen and I carried on, intending to complete our mission. Then, lead a contingent yourself back to see if we can parlay with the people in this wood. A line of communications in the least, trade at best."

Lamorek nodded – this was no discussion. Tristlen and Galaborne dismounted and handed him the reins, "As you win the day and take all the glory yourself."

"When it's retold again and again, we'll skip the mighty steed that toppled his rider part," Tristlen smirked.

"Agreed," Lamorek turned away, Stormblood following without the necessity of a guiding hand.

Galaborne readdressed the mountain entrance, looking down into the black, unfathomable deep. There was a clear stair fashioned from the rock as it descended, "It's been in use recently," Galaermus observed, "Most like our strange friends are ahead."

The riders, horseless now and riders no more, descended into the deep and followed its stair for a long while, losing track of all sense of time. When the stair leveled into a smoother path, sconces of blue flame lit a twisting passage that wound farther into the mountain laterally. When they came to a crossroads, the shaft split into three. What he called north, Galaborne saw was decorated lightly with a tapestry every dozen or so feet – at their angle, he could not see their depictions. To the west, low thrumming sounds as if machinery at work echoed before them, the occasional *ting* of a hammer striking anvil rang out amongst the rest. His attention turned when Tristlen nudged his arm with elbow, "Look," he said, "Do you see it?"

Galaborne spied down the eastern hall, but saw only rock and lamplight.

"The floor," Tristlen guided his captain's eyes.

In the blue firelight, Galaermus spotted it. Fading from the rock floor of their current station, the hall was laid with marble forming a colored mosaic panorama of some great story long passed. Its first chapter he could make out, two great stars falling to Aegis and burning into the depths of the world. "You can see farther than I, which way do we go?" Galaborne asked the archer.

"The mosaic," Tristlen surmised, "It tells the story of creation. Those stars are the Aeonar, the Endless. I was taught their history before my exile. I can see the great rocks of the Dûn'raeor a few feet in."

"Creation's a good place to start, maybe the past will lead us to these people's present."

"My thoughts as well," Tristlen agreed.

Galaborne and Tristlen walked down the aisle of history's beautiful mosaic until it reached tiles that dimmed in comparison to their vibrant ancestors; they were all shades of gray, and puzzled together they showed a people lost in the darkness, manacled together, ankle to ankle. A great fire-breather watched over them spitting a black flame from his maw, though his eyes were of lily white. The imprisoned train of what appeared to be the Shadowalkers faded with each individual, into a mist that in the end consumed them. It grew brighter and brighter until the tiles were as white as cotton, and the whole passage was lined floor to ceiling with a purity greater than even the most virgin linen. The mussed and mess of the two knights looked a deplorable contrast to the passage, and as Galaborne focused from it to Tristlen, then back to the glitter, it felt almost embarrassing, and most positively blinding. Past the hall's end, it opened up into a great atrium beyond either Nûmunyr's wildest dreams.

They stepped in, and saw the entirety of the atrium was calcified and glittering via thin pinhole shafts that shed light in from the exterior. Everything sparkled like the waves of the Silent Sea at dawn. This was not just grand, it was godly. There, they saw six calcific columns that rose in the atrium's center, between each was a short stair leading up a dais to a circular platform that held six thrones. Sitting upon these six thrones were men not unlike the strangers they met in the wood. With the light so magnified, Galaborne would have been able to see straight through them to the opposite side of the room if it hadn't been for the gilded robes. To add to their magnificence, the gilt-leaf fabric was adorned with gems and minerals in a rainbow of vibrant color, fashioned to jeweled perfection in symmetrical patterns with cleaved rings that bedecked every finger; their ears bore links of precious stones barred through and leading down to their shoulders. However, for all their wondrous treasures, Galaborne could hardly swallow his terror – as the robes lay open, he could see their beating hearts through their chests.

"Captain?" Tristlen asked warily, as he had spotted the eerie phenomenon as well. "Be they angels or demons?"

"Ah!" one of the crowned Lords raised a hand, forefinger to the sky – even its nail was painted gold. "Now that," he spread his arms and stood, "is the question."

"Are you the Shadowalkers, the same as the people under the mountain Shadow? We know you by these descriptions alone."

"Aegis calls us the Evendain," the Lord answered. "Those in this ring seated before you are the Lords of the Evendûmn Hall, in which you now stand. Tell us, Nûmunyr, have you come to steal our treasures or take them by force, or do you think you can parley with us? Barter for our riches?"

"I'm not sure to any of that, for I have no certainty as to what it is we seek, or if you have it. If you do not, we simply seek its whereabouts."

"And if we do have it?"

"We are a peaceful people."

The Lord said nothing to this at first; instead, for long moments, he pondered, then sat. Galaborne heard the creaking of bows release their tension slowly from concealed corners of the room. "Tristlen?" Galaermus asked the keen-eyed.

"Aye. We're lucky to be alive, I think."

"Your words interest me; that is where your luck lies. Tell me, Nûmunyr, what does the Thrush-King want of us, this boy that leads you all to his doom?"

"You mistake him for another, m'lord. Our King is a great man, kind and valiant in all his ways."

"What I said stands true as you grow less interesting to me in your blind loyalty to him. He was a boy when he came first to us in a time long away and far ago, and is still so now as we see it. Why are you here?"

"We are on a holy crusade, my Lord. A quest for an object of great symbolic purpose, if not power. The whispers of Aegis came to our King, and have led us to you."

"We have a great many priceless things in our storm-riddled depths, through the fire and lightning if you dare them. Do you have a name for this mysterious treasure?"

"Our liege called it only ... a Heartstone, and fears if we do not find it, much will be lost when a great Shadow befalls our world."

"Ah," the Lord appeared satisfied with Galaborne's answer. "The heart of anything is a great burden. To win such a prize as a lover's warmth, you need far more than courage in your blood or strength in your steel. And to keep such a thing for your own to the end of time is an even greater endeavor. What makes your city so worthy?"

"I cannot attest to what this artifact may lend us, but our people are the beating lifeblood of our worth, and they are true and virtuous and proud to be all that they are. I am merely my King's swordarm, and will find for him what Aegis wants found."

The Lord chuckled, low and deep with subtle vibrations that quivered his guests. "Your King has lied to you, Thrushman."

"May be it, he misinterpreted the vision, but—"

The Lord stood, interrupting Galaborne's defense, "Thane, the Thrush-boy is never lacking of visions or the clear interpretations of such. He knows exactly what Aegis showed him, what you say She wants found. He has been blessed by this curse since the Eighth guided his hand across the Shores. But, I'll grant you this, if She believes the Heartstone of the Wreathe is better in the hands of this boy, let the stone speak for itself and judge. If it so desires another keeper, it shall have you." The Lord took long strides across and down from the dais and stood in front of them, his height grand and foreboding, "Follow me, Nûmunyr."

An entire cycle of Aegis' moons passed on their journey through the dark, in which very little was learned by the riders out of Nûmundor. There was no reckoning of time, but their Evendain Lord grew mortally tired as they, and all rested along the underground road in pockets set every few miles with water and supplies. Some were naturally forming springs, others were fashioned from the rock and made ready for travelers. The Evendain needed to eat and sleep the same as any man, but in the mountain's depths, Galaborne found it uneasy to do either. Eventually, the sconces grew weaker and sparse, until they disappeared entirely.

"Do you not carry a light with you?" Tristlen asked, tracing the passage wall for guidance.

"We follow the Vein, and need no light for that. Aegis takes us where she will, and we are her servants for it. We are not the Fyrzhor, who desecrate her womb with axe and gear."

"But ... what of your ... adornments?" Tristlen pressed.

"We take only what she gives freely," the Lord said with finality.

Silence fell over the company again. At length, they reached a dark stair. As they ascended, it gradually brightened, limestone of lighter colors fading into a new mosaic. This time, the tiles depicted waves and battles and lovers neither Galaborne nor Tristlen recognized. Even the lamps frequented once again as the spire rose high, the stair steeper. Galaborne cocked his head to one side, "Do you hear that?"

"The ocean," Tristlen nodded.

"We are at the far end of the Cascade," the Lord offered.

They passed windows so thin even an arrow could not penetrate their width, the light rent in with glaring overexposure. "I see nothing," Tristlen confirmed the inability to see without before they continued on.

"We climb a citadel, tall and white rising against the sun. Its grandeur is only surmounted by its design. It was built by an unknown people for an unknown purpose. Come."

The company ascended the rest of the stair, and it was sunset by the time it opened up into a large circular room. The floor was tiled much like the mosaic, and the space was filled with mountains of books. "A library?" Tristlen asked.

"A museum anachronistic," the Evendain answered. "Do you know of Mimyr's Athenaeum?"

Galaborne nodded, "It's said to be the birthplace of the written word, and keeps all accounts of it."

"While Mimyr holds history and knowledge, this place holds only mystery. The Athenaeum records the past. This spire accounts something to our understanding unfathomable. We are its keepers."

"Captain," Tristlen nabbed Galaborne's attention.

Galaborne followed Tristlen's gaze to the rafters. Before them, great disc-like stones set a perimeter of a promenade overlooking the room. They magnified with great intensity the sun's rays from measured slits in the stone roof, much like refractions of light off glass.

"Those aren't mirrors, Galaermus."

"They're stones," the Evendain Lord finished for him. "Does one of them call to you as it called to your absent King? Which do you claim as keeper now, Nûmunyr?" he said this scornfully, clearly proud of the duty he thought the Evendain held over this place, unwilling to relinquish it easily.

There was a single ladder in the chamber which took Galaborne and Tristlen to the loft. Set on pedestals around the wooden promenade were thirteen stones, each a different color and hue. On closer inspection, the riders found them only to be the size of a large fist, but their shape and grooves reflected all that struck it – they alone were needed to illuminate the tower. As the riders passed each one, they heard whispers, as if a thousand voices were speaking secrets to one another over a hush and fire. Each crackled lightly, sparking with life through their crystalline structures. "Is this some wizardry, then?" Tristlen asked himself out loud, "Or alchemy?"

"We are not worthy to be in this place," Galaborne admitted.

The Lord stood behind them without warrant, "If you take, so must you give. You must leave your own heart behind if you steal one of theirs."

Galaborne stopped in front of a stone with amber hues. It drew him in like a song, one he couldn't remember the words to, but knew its chords, a lullaby of memories left by the future instead of written in the past. "This is it. The Heartstone of Nûmundor."

"We have nothing, but ourselves," Tristlen hypothesized, "Does one of us stay?"

"Whatever truths our King's vision held, this will save our people at Age's End," Galaermus couldn't take his eyes away from it.

"Your family waits for you," Tristlen said. "I will stay."

At first, Galaborne didn't answer; instead, he was listening. "Do you hear that?"

"Captain?" Tristlen heard nothing tangible.

Galaborne heard it, the whispers, trilling in his mind's eye: *Yes, Knight-Errant. Bold crusader.*

Your journey is done. Take us. Take me and protect your home, your loved ones. I am your answer. There was something about the voice that alarmed Galaborne, but the song was sweet in his ears, his yearning for home growing with each word uttered: *Your wife. Your child. We can make you King. You can protect them forever. Cherish them always under your own rule. I am all there is. I am your heart.*

Tristlen gripped Galaborne's shoulder tight, turning him away from the stone's thrall and ripping him from the fatestream's grasp. "I have no one. I will stay."

Galaermus looked at his friend, shuddered, "I cannot take it. I cannot tell you why. If Aegis wants our Thrush-liege to be its keeper, I cannot take it to him. I will betray him. It knows my heart and has some power over me."

Tristlen looked at the stone, "I don't understand."

Galaermus did, "You have no one, want for little beyond what you already have, so it has no means to sway you. But, it commands. It has its own purpose, Tristlen. Keep it hidden until you enter the Whisperhall. Show it only to the King."

Tristlen addressed Galaborne again, sadness in his eyes, "I will come back, be it my sole purpose, sir. I will be your winged messenger, and I will take care of your family, I promise."

"I expect no less, my friend." Galaborne clasped forearms with his loyal companion, "And I will return to Nûmundor, when this mystery unfolds." Galaborne's eyes shifted to the Evendain.

Tristlen took the stone quick as a heartbeat, for he did not like the feel of it now. He wrapped it in cloth to hide its shine, for he no longer liked its look. Lastly, he emptied one quiver of arrows to drop the Heartstone to the bottom. After its light *thud*, he replaced the arrows, hiding the thing away, then retreated down the stairwell, for he did not wish to wait.

Galaermus didn't have the heart to watch him leave, but questioned the Evendain, "Will you lead him out, m'lord?"

The Evendain kept Galaborne's gaze, "He will find his way. Though it will be long, there is no peril through the Vein. And my people will guide him from the *Everö'vitûm* to the Gatestream."

Galaborne studied the light shining through the Lord's skin, revealing his anger, a heart pumping faster with rage he kept from his face. Casually, Galaborne smirked, then sat down on the promenade's planks and hung his legs over the edge. He kicked the air, "Now, tell me, Evendain. Tell me everything that you're not telling me."

There was a long moment in which the knight-errant thought the mighty being might attempt to kill him. Then, the Evendain Lord sat next to Captain Galaermus Galaborne and smiled.

Anthology I

An Evendain's Exchange

High Lord Zain-evare Fyrön

The Stormstone Cascade

*...being a short story during the Age of Origin,
approximately in the year 819...*

High Lord Zain-evare Fyrön of the
Evendain-evare withheld his wrath as he stared in
contempt at the Nûmunyr captain. He could feel
the sparks behind the embers of his eyes stimulated
by the distemper pulsing through his veins. This
favored and gallant knight who flaunted an air of
righteousness and self-sacrifice threatened the
tempest raging in Fyrön's blood. This boy was no
more than a heathen crusader on a fool's crusade, a
sheep led by a fox to the maw of the wolf. Fyrön sat
down by the lamb's side with a mocking flourish
and smiled to disarm his opponent with a false
pretense of pleasantry. Noticeably, the knight
relaxed. The pair studied their own feet for some
time before the keeper of the *raeordûmn* decided to
confront the fool, "Your King knew what he sent
you to do."

Galaermus Galaborne did not meet the
Lord's gaze. Whether due to the Evendain's visage,
a being of nigh translucency in the light caught and
cast about the room by the Heartstones
surrounding them, or whether it was due to
something else, Zain-evare didn't know. The

knight raised two fingers, "That is the second time you accuse my liege of treachery – or is it the third? Why do you have such derisive distaste for the Thrush-King?"

The Lord knew this knight would be loyal to a fault. He decided to test the captain's knowledge, rather than his heart, "You know nothing of that boy you call King."

Galaborne chuckled, "Have you seen him lately? He is an old man. Quite so. And what I've seen – his hand tremble with the curses of age. Please, enlighten me, milord. What do you see?"

"You are all children in the eyes of the Evendain," Fyrön cooed.

"Heh," to Galaborne, semantics were amusing, "How old are you, then, I wonder?"

The Lord cocked a wry smile, "Physical age is what you presume and ponder; whereas, I speak of understanding."

"Omnipotence is a trait for gods."

"You are impetuous. A tool."

"Aye. I have never doubted that. Thane deserves my service."

"Thane deserves nothing," Zain-evare spat, but stopped himself from elaborating. The Nûmunyr was trying to provoke him, but the secrets of the Evendain would stay locked in their calcific halls. It was time for accusation: "The Thrush-boy desecrates Aegis with his own desire."

This turned Galaborne's head, his own temper rising, "Aegis whispered Her need of him; we only came for Her."

Fyrön leaned in, "Your ignorance is almost frightening."

Galaermus didn't budge, "It's a stone, milord." He leaned back casually, "Frankly, I believe less in the mystical properties of a rock than the belief of our people that our King can talk to birds. Granted, my mind is ever disputing that. However, I do believe in symbols, and if that's what this Heartstone is – for our people in a coming war – that's all I need to know to sacrifice myself for hope."

The Lord matched the captain's posture, "The *raeordûmn* are no rallying cry."

"A mineral, then? A weapon he seeks to forge by breaking it apart on the anvil and smelting it anew?"

"A weapon, indeed," Fyrön shook his head – he knew better. Or at least, the Evendain thought they did. There were mysteries in the Heartstones his people had not dared to investigate. "You heard the *raeordûmn* calling you, heard its voice and shied away from its command. You feared it. And you were right to. Will your King do the same?"

Galaborne looked back at the stones, recalling the one whose whispers strained to corrupt him, "His heart is not as frail as mine. He will do what is best for our people. If Aegis will command him through this thing, let him follow it, I say."

"There lies your misconception, knight."

"Where?"

For a moment, Zain-evare held the crusader's eyes in his own, then he stood and walked the length of the promenade. His eyes fell on each stone in turn, all of different colors and hues and cuts, but turned away before reaching the Cascade's. "The Evendain do not believe the Heartstones are Aegis-born; we do not believe Her womb fashioned their majesty. Theirs are not Her whispers, but another's."

"Whose?"

"We have speculated that answer, but came to one conclusion – it is not a question to be answered."

Galaborne crossed his arms, "Well ... what's the use in that?"

Fyrön guffawed, a booming drum in the hollow citadel, "You Nûmunyr are so arrogant."

"And it would appear the Evendain are cowards."

"How dare you!" the Lord spat, "We walked this world long before your Boy-King was led across the Shores. We were servants of the gods and slaves to the Vein before the twelve races could take hammer to anvil, before the gods forsook us for their newer likeness, their lesser and wretched scions."

"I suppose you never asked them why?"

"You're a blasphemer."

Galaborne finally stood, but his command was diminished by his shorter stature, "I am a man. A Nûmunyr. That is all I claim to be. And my servitude is a choice. One I happily make. Is yours?"

"It is not our place to say."

Galaermus spread his arms, "Why?"

"Because, we were the first, and we will be the last."

Galaborne pointed an accusing finger at the Evendain, "Now, you do sound like a god."

Fyrön shook his head – this man was unbelievable, "You know nothing."

"You're right," his adversary shrugged, "I don't. That's why I ask questions."

There was a silence, long and drawn across the mysterious library. It was unheard of for a Nûmunyr to even be granted an audience with the Evendain, let alone have one question their faith.

Zain-evare knew he shouldn't let this youngling rattle him, but his prattling had awoken some heretic curiosity in the Lord, and it had started him to wonder.

It was Galaborne who broke the silence this time, walking forward: "For example, tell me, which one of these is the Evendain's. You are a people of Aegis, are you not?"

Fyrön paused, then paced. He would either deny the question an answer, or reveal to this knight more than he ought to feed his own internal demagogue. He wasn't sure that it much mattered given the situation, the knight already believed he was a willing captive of the *raeordûmn*. As long as the Heartstone of Nûmundor was in their city, this knight-errant would reside in the Citadel. And in part, that was true; to reveal anything more would either be a miscalculation or a revolution against the Evendain's ancient burden of secrecy.

"You claim to be their keepers... You protect them. It's this one, isn't it," Galaborne mused, yanking Fyrön from his thoughts. He'd reached a stone the color of pitch. Beneath the crystalline shell, he saw the nebulous of obfuscation, a cloudy mirk as if a great mist had settled over a dark land incarcerated within.

Zain-evare answered quietly, "That is the Heartstone of the *Eventyr-aeor*, yes."

"I thought the *raeordûmn* were for peoples, not places," Galaborne pressed.

"They are for the Realms; the Evendain are unsure whether the races of Aegis numbering the same as these stones are by the fatestreams design or by simple coincidence."

"For the Cascade, then, but not the peoples who call this place home?" Galaborne challenged the Lord, "Does it call to you, as ours did me?"

Zain-evare let his eyes drift to the pitch. From this distance, no, of course it didn't. If he walked closer, it would. It would say many terrible things to him, accuse his kind of many terrible deeds done and that which they would still do. It was fraught with the same storms that riddled the Stormstone Cascade. It would light the embers behind his eyes and spark countenance of wrath upon his people's state and place across Aegis, within Aegis. "We were the first, and will be the last. We have no need of such a stone."

"Even if it is the Heart of your people?"

The High Lord Zain-evare raised his voice enough to see fear rise in Galaborne's eyes; the words came scratchy but unassailable, "Look into that stone, knight of virtue, knight of nature's child – tell me you see goodness." Fyrön watched Galaermus twitch – the man was unsure of himself, now – so he continued, "Tell me you see anything beyond Shadow beneath Shadow."

Galaborne looked, but said nothing. Fyrön knew all the knight saw was darkness, pure and deep and black. There was nothing else the stone held.

Zain-evare walked up to Galaborne, taking slow and controlled breaths, readying himself for what was to come, "Now, knight of thrush's vision, would you like to hear the voice of the Stormstone Cascade, the command of the Shadowgourge? Only then can you tell me, Nûmunyr, if this was the Heart of your people, could you accept it, desire it, cherish it for your own."

"I am not afraid," Galaborne responded at length.

Fyrön was behind him now, "As already observed, you are a fool. But even a fool has merit in his own observations." The Lord took the knight's hand beneath his own and placed them both on the *Eventyr'aeor Raeordûmn*.

Immediately, Galaborne attempted to pull away, but Zain-evare clamped him where he stood, hard under his own palm – this was no less painful for the Evendain. He knew the knight saw and felt the same as him in the end:

Emptiness.

It was the acute, striking agony of emptiness. It was throes of torment through a tempest of a clarion abyss. It was the despair and loneliness of nothing.

In the end, Zain-evare released Galaborne when he himself could take no more. When Fyrön stepped away, Galaborne collapsed to his knees. The Lord stared down, almost sorry for the boy, "If it is true that these Heartstones manifest the core of each Realm of Aegis, what does that say of our lashed land under lightning, our mountain deep and beautiful ... what does it say of our people?"

Galaermus pulled himself up, using the timber rail of the promenade to support him. He stared at the High Lord, which unnerved the Evendain how resolute the man's face of stone appeared now. "Then, why don't you change?"

"The stones draw only from the truth, Galaborne."

"Change the truth!" the crusader cried, "You don't have to be cold and empty."

"That. Is our heart."

Galaermus shook his head, "It doesn't have to be."

Fyrön pondered this – to change the Heartstone would be to change the will of a power far beyond mortal kind, possibly beyond Aegis herself and to the *Evar'tûm*. He cocked his head back at the stone.

"You claim to be their keepers, and yet you act like slaves." Galaborne indicted.

Zain-evare placed his hand back on the Heartstone, his eyes lighting again through the waning hours of twilight. He took it from its place on the pedestal.

"I thought a heart had to stay behind for one to be taken for their peoples' own?"

"I lied."

High Lord Zain-evare Fyrön left the crusader there with nothing but the stones around him, the library of tomes and texts below him, and the thought that he could return home without incurring the wrath of some ungodly power. However, he would have to take a guess, a chance against the fatestreams. They would both have to choose very soon how their destinies aligned, sacrificed or sanctified.

A Clansman's Folly

Ahtga, Arcain of the Lynxblood

The Spine of the World

*...being a short story during the Age of Origin,
approximately in the year 850...*

Ahtga the Thinker pondered cross-legged in front of the clan's prisoner. It was his usual posture for an occasion that called for a casuist; however, his personal morality had no place here, under a hanging of stolen hides, draped and drawn to form three walls. Outside the little awning, erected quickly and entirely for this purpose – isolation, Ahtga's kin still bore the sweat of a brow fresh from battle. The Lynxblood's target was an unsuspecting caravan along a route that curved blindly around the mountain – one of the snowcaps which the clan was in the process of taking for their own. Bleda the Mighty dreamed of a day when the whole of the Spine was under the rule of a single man, a man who would unite all clans as one. This venture was their northernmost expansion, risky, but rewarding thus far. Before their prey spotted a single Lynx, it was over: The mountain men sprang from the canopy and brush of the pass without a sound, first taking down the strange, four-legged beasts the passing enemy rode. Afterward, the footmen fell in seconds. The sheer savagery of the clan's offensive defeated the enemy's mind before a single *leyax* tore into their flesh. Now, the blue-eyed, yellow-haired female in front of Ahtga was the single survivor of the cavalcade.

Ahtga, as was his duty as the clan's *arcain*, waited until the battle was over and prisoner taken before he'd come forth from Shadow. Now, it was his responsibility to sieve through the survivor's mind to collect the knowledge his clan could use for future raids. Ahtga already learned the woman's name and place of origin – Irles and Orphaeon. The woman would only die after his use for her was through.

"I don't s'pose that's to heal these little scrapes I have?" Irles asked in jest – the rider kept her humor through the pain of the large gash cut across her forehead and thigh wound received during the battle; blood trickled a red rivulet of iron over her brow and into her eyes, while another river ran deep into the soil. Ahtga was sure it stung, but Irles revealed no discomfort. Her strength would soon falter.

Her question referred to the concoction she watched the Thinker grinding in a small stone bowl between them. As mystic and healer, the *arcain* was to know every root and every rock of Aegis, what they could do, could heal, and could harm. In this Isdûm Cycle, *cailux* was easy enough to find; in fact,

Ahtga discovered a shrub nigh the size of a small tree not far from their camp. Its suckering leaves of perennial stems grew tall and wild this time of year, and the long, reddish-purple stalks faded into dark leaves, green and glossy. Ahtga had plucked away and set aside the deep, ribbed lobes, ignored the inflorescent panicles flowering about it, and peeled straight past an ovoid spike to find the fruit hidden within. Beneath its spring capsule, the *cailux* berthed large oval seeds shining bright, but deadly poisonous. He removed one, dropped it into the bowl and continued grinding. One was all he needed.

Ahtga only stopped to catch Irles' eye with his finger; he poked her heart. With her attention grabbed, he picked a nearby wildflower from the earth and brought it to his lips. The *arcain* blew the little seed tufts one by one from its head in a stream of white bannering on the wind, hoping the motion would resemble a quick rate of decay unto death. Most of what the realms considered civilized people thought the mountain clans knew very little of the El'arria, of the realmspeech. The nomadic tribes liked keeping it that way, for it placed them in a superior position during times like these. They played dumb as a feint.

Irles followed the Thinker's drift, "I s'pose if I don't give you what you want, you'll give me that

– something I'd rather not want," she eyed the bowl. "A poison?"

Ahtga drew his *leyax* from its sheath – it was a short blade, notched on its flat end opposite its curvature, perfect for close encounters, good for ripping out an enemy's entrails once inside; however, now he used it to draw lines in the sand. The shapes and arrows were as clear as painting on rock with mud could possibly define.

"You want to know about my people?" she asked.

Ahtga smiled – she understood.

Irles narrowed her eyes, "My people are the mighty horsemen of the North. My people are tall and proud. My people are greater than you. Your barbaric nature, rudimentary tactics and weapons of bone would do nothing against Orsain cavalry if you ever dared press to our plains." She pointed to the large black beast with four legs she rode in on. "The horse. That will be your end if you come anywhere near our cities."

So, that's what they called it. Ahtga snorted. Other Clans may be foolish enough to make war on the flatlands, but the Lynxblood were merely bold, not stupid. If this place she heralded – Orphaeon – was far from the Spine, he wondered where the soldiers were headed so high up in their passes.

Ahtga cleared his throat; it was time to speak, "Purpose? In mountain?"

"Oh? You're not completely mute, after all? Still, what savage peoples lay waste to a trader's caravan and slaughter innocent people?" Irles looked down, her exhaustion finally showing, "We were only here to trade, nothing more."

With the look of the caravan, the way it was protected by armored riders, Bleda the Mighty assured the clan there were either riches or weapons inside. The former would be valuable for trade in the foothills, the latter for war on the rise. Unfortunately, they'd found nothing more than a small trunk, one his kin were still attempting to open. They would use what they could of the dead's maille, but the spears they carried would do little for the nomads. The men of the mountains fought in close-quarters only. Surprise was their tactic, bone their tool. Bleda believed they were hiding something else, thus the *arcain* was forced to continue, "Purpose?" Ahtga grunted again.

Irles shook her head, "Taking supplies to Myrimill. That's it. What right do you have?"

"Our mountain."

Irles laughed, "You must be mistaken, *ogri*, you've ventured too far north. If your kinsmen lay claim to any mountain, it is not this one. Run back south where you belong."

It was true, Ahtga knew, they were far from home. Bleda the Mighty desired glory, to conquer the great snowcaps. *At what cost*, Ahtga thought, *but no*, his morality had no place here.

"All you will find here, mountain man," the rider continued, "are the gods. Do you believe in those? You better. They will be angry at your transgression."

Religion was for fools. The Clans, no matter their differences, believed in only two things collectively – the *dir-aeor* and the *dir-öt,* the sister moons of Aegis. The *dir-aeor* was she of rock, her properties of stone and mineral gave them their precious gems and hardened their tools. The *dir-öt* was she of root, who gave them their food, medicine, poisons. The *cailux* he mixed was one of her many gifts, and its threat was working well on the woman. When a soldier started going to their gods, they were breaking. The Thinker pressed further, "Purpose?"

"I told you, we're tradesmen!" Irles lost her temper. "Bound for Myrimill! Do you know it? A hop north of here, a skip and a stone's throw from Myrhaven. We have nothing of value to you!"

Ahtga's eyes widened; the clans heard stories of Myrhaven. It was a stronghold with some great treasure kept within some ancient vault. It would be the greatest conquest of their time if the

Lynxblood could take it for their own. All the Spine would bow, and all clans seen knelt before Bleda the Mighty. The *arcain* spread a line of the poisonous solution on a small strip of bark and raised it to Irles' lips, "Purpose."

"I don't understand," the woman pled, her lips trembling. "Please…"

Another Clansman joined them under the private awning and whispered in the Thinker's ear, "Tharga."

Ahtga gave the brute a surprised glance back, but his kinsman just shrugged. Tharga was not the strongest of them by any means, though he may now be called Tharga the Lucky if he was the one that got the thing open. Recomposing himself, Ahtga nodded in acknowledgement – he would soon see what this soldier was hiding. Shortly, he would have no more use of her.

"Those scars," she interrupted the Thinker's thoughts after his kinsman left. "Those weren't of an enemy's blade, were they? There looks to be ceremonial purpose behind their direction."

Either Irles was very observant beyond even clairvoyance, or she knew more about the mountain clans than she eluded to before. She was right, of course, but why did she ask?

"I heard on the road... She who carries you slashes you before you are even allowed a first nip at her milk."

She was gaining a superior position over him now; knowledge was power.

"That is cruel," she continued.

Now was the time to catch her off guard, so he stood and spoke plainly, "From birth, the men of the mountain are taught how to endure pain." Speaking in such a fluent and proper manner did its job; fear crept back into Irles' eyes. There was now a mystery here she had not uncovered.

She trod carefully, eying the *cailux* in her keeper's hand, "There are many things we cannot understand about one another, I think, but I do understand what that is used for. You call it *cailux*. And it will kill me quickly ... after you are done with me. Why not just use your blade?"

"Blade is for battle," Ahtga smiled, "We are not savages."

"And I don't deserve to die. We were carrying nothing of value to you."

Ahtga disregarded her lie, yet again, "This is our mountain, now."

Ahtga's kinsman returned with Tharga; the pair carried a large chest and dropped it at the *arcain's* side. Irles didn't seem to notice or care. She kept her eyes on her keeper. Ahtga waved his kinsmen off; and addressed his captive one last time. Irles' face revealed nothing of the trunk's contents.

Inside, Ahtga found only curiosity. The trunk was filled to its rim with fine-worked pieces of glass, all stained in different vibrant colors. They were treasures of no worth, but their beauty was enamoring. At length, and with a fallen heart, Ahtga's eyes burned again into Irles, "This ... your prize?"

Irles nodded, "Did the men and women you slaughtered deserve to die for it? Do I?"

Ahtga slapped the woman across the face, splitting her cheek with the iron adorning his fingers – this couldn't be it, there had to be more; they were missing something, the caravan had been so well protected, "What's its worth?" It was possible there was some new use in the flatlands for it.

"None. The oracle ordered it fashioned. For use in the next stage of construction in her Athenaeum. Or so we were told. That's all. Two other shipments have already reached Myrimill. One from Templeton and one from Nûmundor. Ours was to complete the desired quantity. You gain nothing here, but the blood of innocents soaking your wild blade."

"This is our mountain, now," Ahtga pushed his forefinger over Irles' bottom teeth and pried open her mouth. He dropped the *cailux* onto her tongue and clamped her jaw shut. He plugged her nostrils with the other hand until she was forced to swallow. She gasped for air as he let her go and exited the awning. It wouldn't take long for the poison to run its course.

Pushing aside his morality, Ahtga crossed the terrain to where his Chief was awaiting the *arcain's* report in the only standing tent they ever brought. Upon entrance, he saw Bleda the Mighty sitting on a wooden seat that acted as the nomadic Chieftain's throne. It was small enough to fit on the back of Rûgila the Dim, Bleda's massive strongarm, during travel. At present, the great mountain man's teeth ripped apart meat taken from the caravan. The spoils of victory, especially when it came to fresh food, went first to the Chief, and only when he was done would they disperse the rest. "What have you discovered, my friend?" he asked through a mouthful of muscle.

Bleda was the one, as a small boy, who bestowed Ahtga the surname of Thinker, for he always caught his cousin offguard lost in deep thought, "The contents of the trunk, locked and guarded... Was there nothing else of value in the caravan?"

"Nay. Now, it's value? What does it offer us or Balymbar the Barter? Is it something we keep or sell?"

"Neither, mighty Chief. It was a religious train, it seems."

"What?!" Bleda spit out the piece he chewed.

"They were transporting a gift to their gods – glass. To the northern stronghold, they call Myrhaven."

"*Aera!*" Bleda threw his treat aside, his temper flaring. "What folly is this?" Bleda paced. "As *arcain*, guide me now. Where does our glory lie, old friend?"

For a moment, Ahtga's mind drifted back to the woman he'd left tied up and dying across the yard. However, the shifting impatience of his liege brought him back to the Chief's attention. Morality had no place in the ebb and flow of a hard life, not in the mountains where every day was fight or die. But that's how life was supposed to be. "I believe we could use this as a rouse. Two more shipments await at the village of Myrimill. We could bring the glass to Myrhaven ourselves in disguise, and once we're inside the city walls, we take the stronghold for our own. It would be the greatest glory any clan could ever dream of. The Spine would bow down before your might."

Bleda pondered this, "And the Myrmen?"

Ahtga shrugged, "Whatever creatures they are, the fairy tales we've heard are most surely exaggerated. They cannot be stronger than we of the Lynxblood."

Bleda nodded, "Then, I will follow your guidance. We will take Mryimill, burn it, leave no survivors that would know of this caravan's disappearance. Then, we'll away north to Myrhaven." He smiled a bronze-toothed smile, "We will take them by surprise, as is our way. Make the necessary preparations, *arcain*."

Ahtga retreated from the tent, but before giving commands to the men, he returned to the awning. Irles was still alive – for now. The *arcain* knelt to the *cailux* and alchemically ground and mixed a second solution, one of opposite purpose. Contrary to its fruit, the plant's leaves could also be a remedy to many things, including its own seed. Once finished, he offered it to the weakening woman, "Myrimill will burn. Save whom you can. But, a warning – if we find no one, there will be no end to Bleda's hunt for them. Take the women, children, alone, but leave the soldiers. They will fight and they will die, but it will be a warrior's death."

She drank the concoction as Ahtga cut loose her binds.

Ahtga stared deep into her eyes, making certain she understood, "Today you live. Go now, and do not look back."

Anthology I

The Myrmen's Might

Zhor, Thirty-Third of Thirty-Three

Mt. Myrkür

*...being a short story during the Age of Origin,
approximately in the year 850...*

Zhor stared at the final letter of thirty-three. The thirty-third represented itself, the *myror* K, the sound *zh*, its name – '*zhor*' – meaning smith. It had etched each letter of the El'arria into stone, casting them for all eternity upon Mimyr's Athenaeum's inner sanctum.

Mimyr the Second was the immortal historian, the keeper of memory, and it was said she found a fallen star on this very site – a star called Myrkûr, who bore into existence the Myrmen for a single purpose: They were to construct a mighty city to store the myths, legends, and histories of Aegis, so that Mimyr need never fear the memories of the world forgotten. Thirty-Three Myrmen were born from Aegis' womb to match the language of the Astar. And while Myrmen was the name spread by the peoples of Aegis, *Myrain* was more precise, for the thirty-three had no gender.

From the threshold of a doorway yet unfinished, came Ama. It was the first of them all, as Zhor was the last. It bore a frown across its stone-like face. All Myrmen were like stone, born of the mountain, and still much a part of it. They were beings of prodigious strength, wide bodied, whose limbs were long and thick as an oak. Ama did not have to draw near, for its voice echoed through the cavernous vault to its end, "There is a woman with a warning without. Ain confirms the rider's northern origin. She claims the shipment of glass bears with it danger."

Zhor met the woman beyond the curtain wall of Myrhaven, far from the reaches of sacristy. As there were so many secrets of the Athenaeum yet to be hidden, few were welcome within the city during construction. The rider fell to her knees and began to plead, "Please, great one, I bring you a warning. Men of the mountain are planning on attacking this holy place."

Zhor raised a hand as large as her head. As it were, Myrmen stood twice as tall and thrice as wide as any other of the First Sires. It fought the urge to smile and asked, "What is your name, child?"

"Irles. Of Orphaeon. In the north, by way of—"

"I know where the city lies. After all, this is the center of knowledge for Aegis herself. Irles ... it means wisdom in sight. The El'arria reveals much to me in your name alone, thus I believe you.

However, have no fear, for we know nothing of it."

"But, they will be disguised. They will—"

"Bring us our glass, will they not? There is nothing they can do to us in this place."

Irles was at a loss for words. It was hard to argue with a being that looked more mountain than mortal, especially as most of the world who'd ever encountered one of the Myrmen saw them nigh as gods as they viewed the Eleven True. The Orsain Horselords were no different.

Sae – sight – called down from the wall, "A company approaches."

Zhor gazed back down to Irles, "Hide yourself, or run. You cannot stay if these men are here for a fight, and we will not give you sanctuary."

"I will fight by your side," she argued.

"You mistake my words. They are here to fight. Not we. There is no *myror* for fight or battle, or even conflict. They will find none of that here. Now go."

Irles was not happy, but she did as she was told, calling back to the god-like creatures, "They are murderers, whether there's a cast for that or not."

Zhor watched her leave. The Myrmen did not judge the races of Aegis. That was not their purpose. Their purpose was to build. *Then again*, Zhor thought, *I am the smith, to forge, and could that not also mean ... to teach?*

Sae kept watch on the wall, looking down at the clansmen, disguised as the long-expected caravan out of Myrimill. They shifted and murmured impatiently at Myrhaven's gates, while thirty-two of the Myrmen sat in the Hall of Council.

The Hall of Council was the first structure erected at Myrhaven, even before the great library was begun, for thought and decision were even more important than records. It was a circular room, one hundred feet high and one hundred feet in diameter. The circumference was ribbed like ripples on a pool of water, giving the stone an organic feel with oceanic vastness. Within this hall, there was discussion, never argument, for Myrmen did not argue, and not a single voice was raised. Ilûm was speaking, "I believe it folly to let these brigands past the gates."

"We have granted all supply caravans a single night to rest within the wall," Myr replied, "As long as they leave by morning, and are watched while they are here. Do we treat these men so differently for one warning that alarms us so little?"

"The Reignman were hit by a blizzard, and the Nûmunyr came a great distance. Weather and circumstance permitted them, and their intent did not bode ill for our cause," Czia said. "They slept the night, then left. What Zhor suggests..."

Vi finished the thought, "What Zhor suggests, we should not even consider."

Pa twiddled its thumbs, something only it was known for when in deep thought, "And what if it is right?"

"They are the simplest of the First Sires," Tûm conjectured.

"The Baymen are more so," Yra corrected.

"Ah, yes, I forgot about them."

"They are easily forgettable," Ûr added.

Eli leaned forward, "Let us not stray from the decision at hand." Eli was the name given to the word 'old' and 'god,' so all listened when it spoke, "What do you think, Isa?"

Isa was it of wisdom, but it stayed quiet, much like Isar the Third herself would have if the Elzhri were here.

Zhor decided to stand, not something usually done by the Myrmen at council, but what it felt was necessary to emphasize its intent, "I truly believe we may have a purpose beyond this Athenaeum. What if we were meant to do more? Not just build, but teach? As the Astar do?"

"We are not the Astar," Rhil trilled.

"We number only thirty-three," Bain added, "The Astar number thousands. It is they who guide Aegis' thought, and the Elzhri who guide the peoples' feet. We are just one of her creations, not one of her makers."

Zhor pressed, "What is this city, but a library? Let us be its teachers. Welcome all races to learn the cast again, as if it were new. How to read and write the *myror* instead of just speak what little is handed down by forefathers who remember the Beginning. Let us not pass through this Age in their eyes as the things that we look, but the minds that we are. As builders we are mute, but we were not born as such, or we would have been born without tongues, without thought, without the ability to hold this council. I have cast the *myror* into stone upon the walls of the inner sanctum, and in seeing them this way, I remembered their purpose. They once brought the world together in a collective shawl of communicative truth. They are not meant to stay in that dark hall."

Dir raised a hand, it was looking at Isa, who had lifted its head and opened its eyes, light reflecting off the glass-like crystals that acted as its irises.

Nga, as it was not all that patient, asked, "What say you, Isa?"

Isa cocked its head, studying the floor, "There may be some wisdom in the smith's words, though not fully reasoned. First, we should take care to never forget – we are not gods. We could be dangerously close to choosing a path not meant for us; however, if we do not try this, we ourselves cannot learn. Therefore, second, I believe we should take one, but only one. The rest must leave. And before they go, the Myrmen will show them what we are capable of, so these savages never return unless called upon."

Each of the Myrmen understood, and there was no further discussion beyond wisdom, beyond Isa.

Wyrd squeezed, its grip on the mountain man's skull clamping quick and sure. The crushing stone fist killed the clansman instantly, while the rest of the disguised in the yard looked on in horror. Their chieftain was dead, and every rumor, every tale they'd heard across the Spine of the mighty Myrmen was found true in that instant.

Ain stepped to the fore, "Who will speak for you?"

Eyes flared with anger, Zhor saw; some, with a debilitating fear. He could see their desire to fight, to kill what executed their liege-lord, but others he saw shook with only one desire – to run. At the end of that terrible moment hanging between war and peace, one brute stepped forward from the host; in his eyes was a glint of understanding calm. "I," he said simply, taking responsibility for his people.

"You will stay," Ain continued, "Your kin will not. This, we command."

The clansman addressed his brothers without argument, "It was a mistake to call this mountain our own. Return south, where we belong, and warn others not to dare the same foolishness, for this story shall now be known, and passed on, as Bleda's Folly."

It did not take long for the host to disappear beyond sight of Myrhaven's wall. Sae rang out the all-clear, and Zhor retreated with this single savage into the holy sanctuary.

Zhor led what it hoped to be its future student down the inner corridors of Myrhaven's Athenaeum - "What are you called?" it asked at length. It was always the first question, for it was the most telling.

"Ahtga," the clansman replied.

"Do you know the meaning of this name?"

"I know what I am," Ahtga answered.

"Do you? The seeds of love that come to an end. That is what you are."

Ahtga scoffed, "A poet's words."

"On the contrary. The El'arria is not for poets. It is truth," Zhor explained.

"I don't understand," Ahtga shook his head, and there was more behind his mask than the curiosity of the Myrmen; there was regret. "Why have you taken me?"

What had this man to regret? Zhor thought. It was a valuable tool in the right hands. "The peoples of Aegis speak a language they do not wholly understand. The speaking of it has been passed down from generation to generation, and much of it has changed since the Beginning. Out of a necessity wroth with desire, they were led astray by greed and avarice, they gave names to violence and death and so much more that saddens the world. And of the El'arria's origin, it is mostly forgotten. The reading and writing of the *myror* is becoming lost." They turned down the hall whose end bore the fateful inscription. "We have a gift for you, Ahtga. For the Myrmen hope that in teaching the truth to one, that all may learn it in time – the magic and wonder of the *myror* – to read, write, and cast the stones."

"The El'arria is said to be the language of gods." Ahtga shrugged, "The clans of the mountain believe little in faith."

"The El'arria is the language of Aegis. If you do not believe in Her, then your people are doomed to pass beyond this age unnoticed." It saw then the fear in Ahtga's eyes. The clansman did not want to be nothing.

When they reached the end of the hall, Zhor

lit a candle and dipped it into a crevice aside the etched alphabet. The whole of the Athenaeum was constructed this way, with series of little pockets connected by thin trenches in the walls that held oil to light the library. After all, one needed light to be enlightened. The flame's course illuminated the letters in a dim, orange glow.

Zhor studied Ahtga, as Ahtga studied the wall. "You will learn to read each *myror*, sound out the letters, and know their meanings. You will learn to cast them yourself and divine what they have to foretell. And if our sires see fit, you will pass the knowledge down the Spine and across all of Aegis, so that all may know its wonders."

"This... I..." Ahtga trailed and stuttered, "I can't."

"You can."

"I am no scholar."

"Do *we* look like scholars?" Zhor asked with its best attempt at sarcasm.

"You are great and powerful."

"Great in stature, yes. Powerful in strength, yes. But, this..." Zhor motioned to the El'arria, "is where the might of the Myrmen rightly lies – the written word."

"It will take years."

"It will take a lifetime."

Ahtga placed his hand on the wall. His fingers

ran over the grooves and curves and shapes, until he truly understood and felt the glory before him. Zhor knew to touch a thing was to know it, as much as to learn it. It made the legend real. Ahtga fell to his knees, submitting to the grand design.

Zhor knew this – the sign of the clansman's acceptance. "We start with this symbol here," Zhor motioned to the wall. "The sound of it is "ah", the very sound that begins your own self, Ahtga. And the name of the *myror* itself is "ama". It means love."

Anthology I

A Wreathelander's Wrath

Maleus, Heir-Apparent and Consul

The Wreatheland

...being a short story during the Age of Origin,
approximately in the year 963...

Maleus was not born a Wreathelander. In truth, he was a Reignman, born Heir-Apparent to the Barony of Templeton, and as such the Consul to Wuhlfsburg. The Barony consisted of six men of excessive wealth and power who ruled over the city-states, and the Consuls were those chosen of the families of the six who kept the laws and laid the taxes to insure peace and tranquility amongst the Reignhearth's oligarchy. It was a highly-civilized way to do things, and the result was growth – the 'Hearth stretched from the Southern Barrows north to the *Czir-aeor Ritûm*, flourishing from the Spine west to the Silent Sea. The Reignmen were educated, refined, and they flaunted it. When the Barony called the thirty-or-so Consuls back to Templeton in the year 953, he found their request surprising: *"We need three of you to gather new lands under the Bells - colonization. You shall seek out savage lands to civilize and bring under our banners,"* they charged. He knew they were in the middle of a rising conflict with the Baymen, and could feel much more transpired behind the scenes, so

Maleus decided to escape it all, and volunteered, one of three, for the holy task. After all, it was a great honor, as the Barony's decree was edict under the Eleven True. The gods were said to have entrusted these men to rule with mercy and love. While there was little of the first and none of the second, Maleus believed in the cause, and wanted no part of another war with the Embers.

Maleus' journey across the Spine of the World was as treacherous as it was uncharted. Three wagons of his lengthy train, well-provisioned and prepared for any encounter as far as the Barony was concerned, were lost in the mountains. The Consul supposed that was to be expected. However, they did not expect the brutality in which the feral mountain clans would prey on them. The savages were easy enough to dispatch, but their barbaric tactics left the expedition little sleep through long cycles. Bad weather and the chance skirmish sped their pace, until they finally rolled down and out of the lower passes of the Spine; here, they found a small village in the mountains' eastern foothills. They buried their dead, and asked for directions. Maleus sought a city of power – they needed to befriend whomever ruled here across the mountains, enthrall them. A shepherd pointed them east, and told a tale of a great city upon a prosperous conflux uniting two mighty rivers.

Therefore, the caravan carried on across fiefs and farmland stretching long and wide until they reached this beacon of light called Mistleton.

And Maleus was sorely disappointed.

This "great city" was no more than a large village supported by stilts and protected by thatch, its people were no more than croppers, herders, and drunks. The only truth to the shepherd's tale was the fact that it was laid out haphazardly over four quadrants within the convergence of two rivers – the North and South Wreathe – whose waters constantly drowned the lower streets in the event of all-too-common rainfall. The Wreathe Rivers wove and conjoined around spreads of swampy overgrowth where every structure was built on platforms that rose above the muddy banks. At the conflux's perimeter, the waters were wide and deep, but they shallowed through the center and between the minute atolls to support whatever these people called their life.

Whilst Maleus was disenchanted, he refused to let he and his men be disheartened. This was an opportunity. The compliment of his caravan was worth more than the entire village; consequently, instead of using it for the expedition's original intent – to trade and befriend – Maleus set himself up as nigh a god, a lord upon the only hill whose crest looked down on the rest of the conflux. The stone they'd brought was used to construct his villa, and the marble fashioned it. The lavish quarter spared no expense; he used the entire trade convoy at his disposal to erect a manor of luxury no Wreathelander could fantasize in his wildest dream. He would sway these people to his cause by either greatness or fear. He didn't care which, for the result was the same – assimilation. In the end, he was here as a Consul of the Reignhearth, nothing more.

As soon as he was settled, he sent a jack to Templeton to explain the situation with only a little exaggeration on the land's value. It took half a year for the Barony to respond. They offered congratulations on his discovery, and looked forward to seeing its fruition as the 'Hearth's foundation in the eastern realms. They'd also informed him of his comrades' fate – placing greater pressure on Maleus' own success. The jackdaw's letter told of Nolthyr, who breached the mountains north and found a place called the Fields of Eurymyr. Unfortunately, it was already united and formidable under a banner of horse and anvil. To conquer this land, they would need to organize a crusade no doubt foolish in its waste of men, supplies, and effort. Then, there was Oleus, the Consul sent south. He'd simply never returned. The man and his train disappeared somewhere beyond the Viridian. All of this and more assured Maleus' resolution to stay in Mistleton. No matter its coarse and artless ways, he'd do whatever it took to educate them in a Reignman's way of life, to make them ready for the Barony.

And much had changed since he arrived.

At first, they mistrusted him, and Maleus anxiously won over their Lordguard. During his transitional rise to power, he was no fool, and knew he needed protection. His own men from Templeton were loyal through and through, and he'd inserted them into the majority of the positions; however, they were not enough. The rest were Wreathelanders who Maleus found would follow him for coin, and the superior living condition granted for quartering in his estate. When there were disputes in the fields, Wreathelanders were used to quell Wreathelanders; when fights broke out in the local bars, the Lordguard put an end to them quickly; when there were attempts on Maleus' life, none succeeded. In time, most of the men brought from Templeton passed into Shadow, from disease or from disaster, and the Lordguard now consisted solely of Wreathelanders who respected him, even loved him as a brother, but they never stopped getting paid.

It was ten years to the day of Maleus' first footfall on the mired, uncivilized conflux, but when he looked out from his balcony, he saw a town in order, finally ready to be handed over to the Wreatheland's new masters. The peasantry would follow the pageantry, and everyone was eating out of the palm of his hand.

Maleus stood waiting on the Wayward Bridge, the western allowance to the conflux. There were four of these bridges that spanned the deep perimeter to the mainland – to the east, the Lyrbridge took the road to a mystical and faithless city called Nûmundor; to the south, the Mireward led to the Wreathemire, where their bonding pitch and tar was bought; and to the north lay the Stormbridge, the breaker of tempests that rolled in from the Stormstone Cascade. The storms that swept in from the north cut in quite hazardously through Mistleton at times, and the rains that resulted would flood the river with a strength that stole away anything in the village not fastened down. The Lordguard took turns securing these ties a few days each cycle. Strong, steel pins kept the bridges in place, and could hold against any rapid; however, if the pins were ever removed, the bridges would simply collapse. Malus saw this flaw, and couldn't imagine why the Wreathelanders built them this way; he never did put much stock in their intelligence. They probably didn't realize the danger to the village if the bridges went out – they would be cut off from the outside world completely, no way in or out. In ten years, Maleus had yet to see a tide low enough for anyone to swim from shore to shore, unless drowning was their desire. The flow from the north converged violently with the flow from the south, causing a clash of undercurrents that would drag the mightiest man under. It was a phenomenon in its own beautiful way, Maleus thought, possibly the only beauty in the whole Wreatheland.

"Tyreus! They sent you?" Maleus greeted his cousin with open arms. The Barony sent family – interesting.

"I was the only one crazy enough to believe you. After all this time, and what happened with Nolthyr, then to Oleus. We'd nigh given up on you."

Maleus rose a brow accusingly, "You're the only Baron left not too fat to sit a horse, aren't you?"

Tyreus grinned, "Yes, I am. I think that's why they chose me to replace Baron Praleus."

The friends laughed and embraced again before Maleus led Tyreus through the streets of Mistleton, bustling with early morning chores. "Once a Consul, now a Baron; Heir-Apparent, now a man of his own. What happened to Praleus?" Maleus asked.

Tyreus shrugged, "Died. Before your jack, we despaired, thought there was no hope of further expansion. So, we decided to really look at what we already had. What we found was enlightening. The old lard was killed in one of a dozen uprisings we've had over the years. None with the means or heart to follow through in the end, mind you. They're all buried round the Barrows, now."

"Buried?" Maleus asked, concerned. It was uncommon to bury the dead.

"Only a few hundred," Tyreus admitted casually. "Traitors don't deserve the *dain'rhil.*"

"How unfortunate." The Reignhearth was not so brutal when he left it, and it was disconcerting to hear his friend talk of the death of their people with such ease.

"They weren't with Templeton. Were rabble. And looked much like most of the people I see here," Tyreus frowned.

Maleus nodded. "Yes, they are quite simple." Maleus eyed the train following his cousin, "I see you brought little company." A caravan so small meant one of two things – they thought taking Mistleton, securing the Wreatheland under the name of the Barony, was going to be just that easy, or they decided Maleus had spent far too long here, and was bringing him home. If that was the case, dead or alive was the important question, now. No matter how long a time he'd been gone, Maleus still held the rank of Consul, even if it was just a title after these absent years; he could only hope it still meant something to Templeton.

Tyreus wasn't stupid; he knew what went through his blood's mind, "Don't worry, my friend, we always wanted you back alive. After what happened to the other two... And you, a Consul promoted to Lord, I see?"

"Self-titled," Maleus reminded him, "to be certain of standing. Chain of command and all."

"We simply don't understand your time frame," Tyreus couldn't care less about whatever politics Maleus was forced to set up to cull the croppers.

"You're worried about my loyalties?"

"Priorities," he corrected cordially, "Priorities."

"Have no fear," Maleus steadied himself, "I am as far from their friend as their rotting homes are from my stone villa. However, I sent for you, because they finally trust my judgement. I believe if the Barony made their push now, the banner of the Bells could be flying over every home across the Wreatheland in less than six cycles time. Just in time for planting season and the rotation of the crop. Though uncivilized as they are, these Wreathelanders are far more advanced than us in their agricultural techniques. We could learn much from them, integrate that knowledge throughout the Reignhearth."

"Ha!" Tyreus bellowed. "Expanding the Reignhearth east of the Spine is progressive and needed, but do not think we would allow their culture, or lack of one, to poison our own – that is neither what the Barony wishes to hear, nor what they sent your expedition this far out to do. They waited long and patiently for you, Maleus. It's time to give them their conquest."

There it was. The Barony had become restless. The Reignhearth was booming, and now it was time to conquer. *It's all for the better,* Maleus thought. The Wreathelanders needed this evolution.

Maleus led Tyreus to the observation balcony of his villa. They stood looking out at the rest of Mistleton and beyond. The village was simple and unimpressive, but Maleus' eyes found the horizon unsettling.

Afar, he knew the Bells of Templeton sung in the morning hues, but past their song, farther northwest than the very borders of the Reignhearth he conjectured, was a gathering of clouds blacker than night itself. He couldn't tell if it were smoke or storm, or some distant wizardry he dared not ponder, but it was deeper and darker than a starless mantle past emberfall. Contrary to this – drastically so – the skies in the southeast over the *Ildûm'tyr Ritûm* were lit up in an orange glow whose rising eruptions and sheer magnitude of volcanic activity meant only one thing: The fires of the forges in the bowels of Seerhold were lit. War brewed.

The Fyrzhor, the grim and private peoples of Seerhold, had a strange eye on the world, a kind of futuresight no one understood. They felt disturbances through Aegis' womb as if they were in direct council with the Eleven True. The black race was the biggest mystery of the east, and Maleus had yet to meet a man or woman who'd ever seen one. If whatever darkness clouded the west could reach as far east as the Ildûm'tyr to light the fires of the Ilaeon, there was something dire about it indeed. He didn't like to think long on it; if there was to be war, it surely would keep far from the neutral, unassuming Wreatheland.

"Is there something you're not telling me, Tyreus?" he asked his cousin.

"You are right, Maleus," Tyreus smiled, avoiding the question, staring out across the backwater village, "They are ready to be culled.

After our failures in the north and south, you've done Templeton proud here in the east. The Barons will welcome you back with open arms and a fat purse if we can pull this off."

Maleus was surprised to feel a twinge of sadness pluck at his heartstrings at the notion of returning to Templeton. *Returning home*, he thought. Templeton was still his home. The Wreathelanders were not a bad people, but he was not a Wreathelander. He was a Reignman, through and through. And yet, the simplicity that drove him to despise the culture, warmed his heart now as he watched a cropper go from door to door—

"Would you look at that?" Tyreus pointed to the man, interrupting Maleus' own thoughts on him. The cropper was going from home to shop, knocking, then being turned away. "Despicable. They even have beggars when there's barely enough to beg for in the first place."

Tyreus was wrong in every way, but Maleus said nothing. He couldn't. In fact, the beggar was a farmer from the outer fiefs – Old Man Cantor, he was called, son of another, dead, Old Man Cantor – and his crop had been destroyed by a *kömn* swarm before harvest. Now, he went door to door offering his hand through the Withering Season and Dûntide, until his own fields could be resewn. It was a proud practice, and in a way bonded the village with the fields surrounding it. There was a trust between Wreathelanders that fouled greed. It also kept people from starving. Finally, a family of four took the man in graciously.

"I would never!" Tyreus spat. "Would you?"

It was a test, and Maleus knew he should not hesitate if he ever wanted to return to Templeton. *To return home,* he corrected his thought. "No. It's disgusting," he lied.

"We will break them of their poverty, give them propriety. We will educate them to live with respect, dignity, decorum."

Maleus knew the Wreathelanders would not respond well to change, as it took them ten years to accept even a single man with such a different philosophy. Enough trusted him now to follow his decree as law, and that would need to do, so he prayed to the Eighth he was doing the right thing. *I am doing this for Templeton, for the Reignhearth, to unify Aegis under one rule.*

"What's that?" Tyreus asked.

Maleus saw it before his cousin. His heart raced, eyes scanning the outskirts – a smoke rose beyond the village, and it was spreading.

"Ha! One of them must have accidentally set his own fields ablaze. Incompetence. We'll break—"

Maleus didn't hear the rest of his cousin's assault on the Wreathelanders fare. He took off, bounding down the villa's grand stair and out the door. Tyreus would never understand the small amount of respect Maleus just realized himself that he had for these people. He wouldn't go so far as to call it care or love. But, it was respect.

"Let them pass!" Maleus called out to the Lordguard barring two Wreathelanders at the outer gate of his villa. The Lordguard stepped back, and the pair collapsed in a frenzy – one a cropper, one a smith.

"Lord Maleus, something..." the cropper started, stuttering.

"Something is upon us," the smith finished. "It's attacking the northern fiefs; the northern fields are ablaze. They will reach the city soon."

"The fires?"

"The creatures."

"What are they?"

The pair of commoners looked at each other, but couldn't find the words.

Maleus knew it was the war, but what for? He knew not the cause, and couldn't imagine it having anything to do with Mistleton. "Do we know what they want?"

The smith shook his head, "They spread chaos with no direction, no formation. They appear to burn for the sake of the fire that ignites in their daemon eyes."

"Let it burn," Tyreus caught up to Maleus, stood next to his cousin and gazed down at the Wreathelanders. Maleus could almost taste the bile in his friend's mouth as Tyreus scoffed, "It will give us less work to do for the Bells. The Barony back home does seem to favor ease over trial and tribulation."

The cropper was aghast, but had no idea who Tyreus was, so continued to plead to Maleus, "Please, Lord. Your home is burning."

Home... Maleus heard the word; they both used it, but were talking of two very different places. *I am a Reignman, am I not?* He saw a plume of fire bellow from the barley leas too close for comfort. Villagers were already taking to the streets en masse with what little weaponry they had – harpoons and butchers' knives. Old Man Cantor stood a head taller than the rest, now that he was alert and erect. He was the only one among the throng with an iron blade.

Maleus turned to his Lordguard, "Sound the *floodhorn* – bring everyone into the safety of the conflux."

"Milord?" one questioned, hesitant.

Maleus knew his cousin's eyes bore into him, but he ignored them, swallowing his fear of consequences in lieu of common sense and saving lives. "We wait as long as we can, then destroy the bridges."

"Pull the pins?" the smith was bewildered.

"Aye. The river will protect us. If fire is their ally, let our water's course be their foe."

Dozens of men, women and children fled over the Stormbridge into the protection of Mistleton. In the distance, Maleus saw the attackers; or at least, he saw where their attacks were taking place beneath the tallgrass. The Wreathelanders disappeared beneath the brush one by one, cut down from below like stalks in the harvest. It was a slaughter. If the things overtook the refugees, he would be forced to pull the pins sooner, and so many would be left behind. Tyreus had kept pace with him when he pushed through the streets to the edge of the Stormbridge, and Maleus saw something horrible in his cousin's eyes – recognition. "You've seen this before?"

Tyreus fidgeted, but didn't answer.

"Tyreus. Tyreus, tell me. What are they?"

Tyreus gritted his teeth, "Seen them? No. The Barony is not on the front lines."

"The front lines of what?!"

"War. From the Embers, but... It's more than that. The tactics we've seen are not the Baymen, yet they fight for whatever else is behind them..." he trailed off. "Most call them abominations, for lack of a better word." Tyreus' eyes met Maleus', "You must destroy that bridge. Now. Right now."

Maleus shook his head, "There are still people out there."

"They're farmers!" Tyreus threw out his arms, "Let them die; they can be replaced. We'll bring true and loyal tenders from Templeton, that wouldn't let their homes burn at the flick of a match like these useless wretches. You are a Reignman, a Consul to the Bells, are you not?"

Maleus swallowed; he knew the Lordguard's eyes were upon him, awaiting his orders. They would follow him without question. He blinked away the tears and looked through their own – he saw something in their eyes he'd never seen before – faith. One last group of refugees approached the bridge. They were dozens. Unfortunately, the creatures were upon them, among their ranks, tearing through them as they flew.

"Destroy the bridge, Maleus!" Tyreus shook his cousin by the shoulders.

Maleus pulled away. "Lordguard! On me!" he ordered, drawing his steel, Templeton-forged, and charged. His Lordguard was not behind him, but beside him.

Maleus and his Lordguard moved into formation – an unbreakable line on the Stormbridge, six in all, as the croppers and tillers of the fields rushed past them to safety. It wasn't long before the abominations – the only description fitting – were in the mix, and Maleus struck a blow into the reptilian scalp of the first one that barreled into him. Its bulbous eyes, somehow inset and askew, were crushed under the Consul's heavy hand. Indeed, abominations was the word. Many were reptilian, others birdlike, some reaching the height of a man, and some shrunk to the size of *wuhlf* cubs. They were terrors pulled from torment, grotesque and deadly, creatures that could've been ripped from Noxukûr's circus itself, a five-ring horror led by the succubus of nightmares. Was she sending her wrath down upon the world, or was this something else, something darker and more terrible than he could believe, assaulting the realms.

When the last of the living were beyond the Stormbridge, and all Maleus saw was darkness and death, he called out to the farmers who stopped to fight by his side, "Go! Pull the pins!"

"Don't you dare!" it was Tyreus, calling up from the crowd, but staying far back from the threshold of battle.

The farmers didn't hesitate to retreat on impulse of order, but when they saw Maleus and his Lordguard stay to keep the abominations at bay, one called back, "Milord. Please!"

"Pull the pins!" Maleus cried. They were already losing ground on the bridge. One snakelike creature slipped past him, but Maleus whirled around to catch it. Exposing his back to the rest of the enemy, he slashed through the snake on the breach. He felt something cold rend through his thigh. The pain brought violence to his vocal chords, and he screamed through the flush in his vision. He spun back to the horde, and his wrath tore through two more. Before he knew it, Maleus was on his knees, and he saw one of his Lordguard dead beside him. "Do it!" he cried out desperately. "I can swim!" he lied. Of course, he could swim, but he wore armor forged similarly to his sword, by the haughty smiths of Templeton – it was strong, and dreadfully heavy; it would sink him to the bottom of the Wreathes. Sadly, his Lordguard were blessed with the same gift, one Maleus had personally given to each, bestowed upon them when they swore their oaths to his Lordship. *Now, they will die for me. Because of me.*

The bridge collapsed, the pins pulled.

Even as Maleus hit the water and began to sink, he felt a pair of massive arms wrap around him. Someone had jumped into the conflux, and now the rapids had them both. However, Maleus promptly realized they were not being dragged under, but drawn back. The arms around him were attached to a body that was tied about the waist and arms by a thick riverboat ropeline. Hand over hand, the Wreathelanders pulled him closer to Mistleton's shore. It was Old Man Cantor whose arms gripped him tight, and it was Old Man Cantor who heaved Maleus over the street ledge to safety.

Maleus' coughing fit lasted minutes before he could properly thank the refugees. This came as a gracious nod alone; appearances and propriety still needed to be kept. He couldn't reveal how hard it was to breath, let alone speak, in his relief to be alive. When he looked back across the water, the abominations on the bridge had been swept away with his Lordguard – the people chose to save him, instead – but there was a daemon host that had reached the border. They cried out in anger or annoyance; they either feared the water, or they thought it a waste of time. He couldn't say or care which, as long as it kept them away from the village.

A young tanner pushed through the refugees gathered around and ran up to Maleus. The boy knelt, "Milord, the pins were pulled at the Lyrbridge as well, but the western and southern crossings have yet to spot this evil."

Maleus steadied his breathing and cleared his throat, "Be ready if they do; try to gather as much food and provision from the southern fields as you can and bring it into the conflux, while we make ready the town."

"Aye, milord." The tanner stood and retreated.

A shriek echoed across the river. One of the abominations, smaller, yet somehow more sinister than the rest, pushed through the ranks of darkness. It sniffed the muddy banks, and shook its head, repulsed. It tore off the arm of another nearby, sheared it straight from the shoulder, then stripped the bone of its flesh to bare the muscle and sinew. The greenish-blue liquid that spilt from the severed arm at the victim's empty joint scorched the earth. The shrieker struck the bone against a nearby stone, and sparks flew. It smiled a ghastly grin, and struck the bone again and again, quicker and quicker, until the sparks lit the surrounding tallgrass asunder. The flames spread quick and fierce across the shoreline.

Maleus knew the northern fields were lost. His only hope was that they could hole up and defend the conflux until someone came to their rescue. *For now,* he thought, *we are safe. For now...* He prayed to the Eighth it would last. Then, he felt Tyreus' eyes on him again. The Baron hadn't moved – the knowledge hadn't escaped him: He was stuck in this backwater, uncivilized village until whatever war that ravaged the realms was won. Or lost... Maleus held out a hand to his better, his superior, cousin and friend, "My name is Lord Maleus. I am a Wreathelander. Welcome to Mistleton."

A Fyrzhor's Fate

Kirdûrikasdûmn, Fyrdûr

Ilsûr'vitûm

...being a short story during the Age of Origin,
approximately in the year 966...

Kirdûrikasdûmn's hand, leathered with age, and fingers adorned with bands of black and white leather, no rings with gem or jewel to flaunt his station, gripped the armrest of his throne. He was not seated atop it, rather standing beside the slab, leaning over it; his head was tilted down, eyes closed, feigning deep thought. The Fyrdûr's simple seat of power, stone and cold, prickled Kirkas' skin with the wintry subtleties of the stone's spirit, the same as were in the thin crown of *myrotûm* cresting his head, cool on his temple. He breathed in and out deeply; it was getting harder of late. Regrettably, the truth was clear – he had not the heart to look his men in the eye to share his despair. They were waiting for a miracle, a revelation of kingly design to save them from the drums – *boom-doom-boom* – they could hear them even now through the halls and heights of Seerhold. They were coming. He needed to make a decision. He needed to make it now.

The king whispered under his breath, a question, rasp and curt, directed to the figure in Shadow behind the dais, "Will you help us?"

The figure didn't move, "No."

Kirkas held back a bout of coughing and grumbled, "Where did they come from?"

"Wrath. Valor. And the Shadow of nightmares."

The Fyrzhor read through riddles as pebbles beneath the ripples of the *Ilsûr-hil*, often unclear beneath the surface, but easy to snatch up if focused on. Sighing quietly, he resigned; there was no use trying to sway a god, especially the Ninth. The Fyrzhor were on their own.

Boom-doom-boom. They were not so far away, now.

Instead of addressing the soldiers behind him, he decided to take his decision to the overlook. From that vantage alone would he accept their fate. He hiked up a winding flight of stairs that wrapped around the exterior of Seerhold's keep tower until he reached the precipice of the stronghold, the highest point in all the Realm. Only Köslûm would follow; the rest of the council of arms would remain in the throne room.

The platform was flat and open, crenelated at its perimeter, but low, as the Fyrzhor themselves grew no taller than a meter or so. They were a short, but stocky peoples, stout and strong with thick beards and thicker guts – both in stomach and resolve. They lived most of their lives in the dark, in tunnels they delved through the mountains of their home. Beneath the Ildûm'tyr were caverns rich with life, cities fashioned and forged by fire and metal, until its beauty could blind the gods. Or at least, Kirkas liked to think so. Those cities of wonder would fall if the enemy found the Deeping Gate along the border.

Köslûm, or Kösnyrilûmdir at its length in the El'arria, appeared behind the Fyrdûr. Köslûm was Kirkas' right hand; as children, no one could tear them apart, or tell them apart, in neither deeds nor disasters. This was before Kirkas was anointed. Things changed after that, but now he had to say goodbye. Together, they scanned the horizon.

From this elevation on Seerhold's precipice, they could see clearly in every direction across the domain's entirety, but only one bearing mattered – north. There, the *Ilsûr'vitûm* was aglow. One fire caught to the next in waves across the woodland; it would not stop, the leaves of that fare too dry. The sun would set soon, and there would be nothing but ash left beyond the Withered Deep to mark the borders of the *ritûm*. That alone, the Ildûm'tyr's volcanic expanse, rose between the enemy and Seerhold, but the distance was diminishing quickly.

There was but a single pass through the mountains to the capital; however, Kirkas had a feeling these creatures needed no pass. They would swarm over the mountains as insects across the field until they hit the tower on all sides. Here, the open Bellows waited, the road to the Cinderstride and the cities of his home. He prayed to the Ninth they could buy his people enough time to escape.

Kirkas, as Fyrdûr, was first to speak, "The Wreatheland. They've burned her fields and salted her soil. The moons have cycled, and yet no jack from Mirestead, Mistleton, or Nûmundor. I fear they may be lost, as I see the bedlam at our borders."

"They have no direction, no desire, my liege," Köslûm replied.

"Oh, no. They have desire. Much of it."

"Have you seen through the *myror*?"

"I have seen with my eyes. Look with yours."

Köslûm looked, but said nothing.

"They desire Chaos. Nothing more. And that is a powerful thing."

There was a long moment of silence. The winds nipped at their cloaks, a precious line of obsidian shimmering at their trims. "How many?"

Kirkas would not answer that question. There were not dozens or hundreds, or even thousands. They were endless, pulled and bred from Noxukûr's circus, if the Ninth's riddle was true and believed, for one purpose – to burn. "Lead the *ildaini* from the Bellows. I will defend Seerhold, buy time for you to ready the ships to take our sons away. If they reach you, brother, then I have failed, and Seerhold has fallen. If they reach you..."

"Set sail," Köslûm finished. He clasped his brother's arm and nodded. "Fight on."

"Stand tall," Kirkas nodded in turn.

Köslûm retreated from the summit without looking back. The Fyrdûr, his brother, was doing the right thing, and it broke his heart. It wasn't a choice, but a responsibility, because the odds of winning this battle were slim to none, and the sons of the Fyrzhor needed time to escape. If the enemy killed the King and took the tower, there was no hope left for the Cinderstride. Kirkas needed to know that his people were safe, and that trust could only be placed in Köslûm. Both brothers would fight to their dying breaths and beyond to give their kin a chance, to take the black ships from the ring, to set sail unto unknown lands across uncharted seas in the hopes that Chaos would not follow.

Would it?

Kirkas stared out over the Ildûm'tyr lost in thoughts of a wayfarer's history and the legends of the Fyrzhor. He could feel the Ninth's presence behind him, felt his own fury bolster because of the Wrathlord's nature, an anger waring with his heart at sending his brother away. "These abominations at our borders, nearing our gates... I have a question, but am pressed to find the words."

The Ninth joined Kirkas at the crenellation, but waited for the Fyrdûr to finish his conjecture.

Kirkas continued, "I have seen the scars they cut through Aegis' body; I have heard her agony on the wind; I have felt the tremor of disquiet through her womb. Of Wrath and Valor bleed nightmares..."

The Ninth silently studied the Fyrzhor.

"In my sleep, I heard Her whisper. Whilst this evil is ravaging Her people and raping Her land, all I hear is shame in Her voice. My question is this, Wrathlord: What does Aegis have to feel ashamed of?"

"Us," the Ninth watched one of a dozen active volcanoes on the horizon erupt violently, shaking the foundry of Seerhold.

Kirkas shifted, turned to look up at the cloaked figure. The god that rose seven feet appeared diminished. The Fyrdûr couldn't believe his eyes any more than his ears. "The Eleven True? But ... you are..." he trailed off. The Ninth had dwelt with the Fyrzhor a long time, and no one ever asked why. After all, he was a god. One doesn't question a god for any reason. Was this his reason?

"The Eleven True is such as it is – wrong," the Ninth answered at length. "There is a Twelfth. Our mistake."

"Another god? A false one?"

"Nay. He is as true as we, but wrong. Our penitence for the Bloodwash. We call him Syrsevar."

"And this fire is his?"

"Indeed. Noxukûr is imprisoned, and he uses her circus to feed his desire."

"Chaos."

The Ninth nodded. "You will fight. This battle is one of six that will define the world of mortals not just as who you are, but who you will become. Far away, the end of Origin draws near. The Evar'nûm bleeds, but its light will shine on, and the Dûn'raeor calls to a Nameless King."

Kirkas pondered long and hard on these things, but only one question pressed through his thoughts, "Is there still hope for us? Will we fail?"

"It is very possible. As your people, mighty and proud say: Fight on. Stand tall. Your fate is up to you."

Fyrnûr Bay was a massive cul-de-sac of docks, aligned as a ring of black berths for trade and travel with only one way in or out – the Paldûm Passage. This channel was a short and narrow flow, wide enough for two brigs at most to sail side by side, no more. Across its breadth was the greatest achievement of Fyrzhor ingenuity – a mighty retaining wall hinged to the Rûkas'war at the foot of the mountains where they met the sea. This defensive giant could open or close the maw of the bay in a matter of minutes with the mechanical *ilgri*-powered axis. While presently it was open, it would stay that way only long enough for every ship at berth to escape. The Fyrzhor who stayed behind to close it would die. A steel catwalk connected the Rûkas'war to its twin – the Lûmryn'war – whose steel spire rose menacingly from a sandbar jutting out from the mainland to the center of the bay. The beacon tower was an island of light that not only guided ships into the bay, but directed traffic within. Here, Köslûm stood, controlling the four sets of mirrors. The glass reflected the sun to cast beams of light down as silent orders, a visual second-language all Fyrzhor quartermasters knew. The signals would follow that line of command from mate to captain to citizen.

Under normal circumstances, if war threatened the Withered Deep, the Western Rim, or the Bay, the Cinder Daughters would take the *ildaini* – the sons of the Fyrzhor – deep into the

Bellows, bar the gates and hole-up until the soldiers far above won out. This time was different. This time, if the swarms took Seerhold, they would breach the Bellows and flood the shafts, an unholy rampage through the Cinderstride. Anyone with the means to leave was ordered to do so; Köslûm refused to imagine how many would be left behind. The truth was the Fyrzhor were not a sea-faring people; the dozens of barges and brigs making ready to disembark at the first sign of trouble would not hold the hundreds of refugees overflowing the wharves. A retreat like this was something their people never prepared for.

In a moment's respite, he caught a glimpse of Seerhold through the clouds, a dark pinnacle of hope against a darker horizon of gloom. He feared the world would soon be lost. He scanned back over the ships at berth. *There must be another way.*

Fyrzhor steel was the finest in the Realms, and the plate suited for the Fyrdûr reflected a smith's perfection from head to toe. However, there was no helmet resting above his gorget; instead, it was a belief of all Fyrzhor their faces needed to be seen clearly by an enemy, ferocity witnessed in the eyes. Additionally, a Fyrzhor's beard was so thick, solidly coiled in firm braids, it acted as a natural ventail, taking the place of maille usually fastened to a coif across the mouth and neck. Without these restrictions, the head was free to turn and address any enemy at any angle, and the sight was clear to catch every attack. It was only below the neck, the plates fashioned in the fires of the Ilaeon began their legendary defense.

Boom-doom-boom. They were getting closer.

Kirkas' pauldrons were broad across his shoulders, matching the width of him. These linked down each side's rerebrace shielding his upper canon. At his bicep, a line of hammers was etched in a descending ring around the plate down his arm. Four thick straps of leather jointed the braces to the steel couter at his elbow, so his axe could swing as it pleased. The hammers marked his family line, each a holy mark of a long dead king, until it reached the fleur-de-lis of his father at the end of his vambrace defending his forearm. His own hammer would be etched into his heir's plate upon anointment. His son would be the youngest Fyrdûr of the Age, but he knew Köslûm would teach him well.

Etched into the back plate of his gauntlet was the anvil. Every time he struck down a foe, it was as if each of his forefathers' hammers came down on that anvil, canon to fist, an exemplification of the Ilaeon itself, to fell them. The fires of that holy forge were also intricately woven up the rest of his plate's design, rising from toe to breast.

Instead of a breastplate – ordinarily a single piece of metal formed to the chest in front to clasp a single backplate – each Fyrzhor bore a coat of smaller plates. These plates were so layered they gave no room for an assault of lance or blade. In turn, those layers were folded in a way that made them twice as thick as Nûmunyr iron, and thrice as reliable as anything the Wreathelanders scavenged. This coat of plates permitted a Fyrzhor to turn at the waist and the shoulders separately, something no other Realm had yet discovered in their slow and cumbersome deathtraps. Beyond that, a Fyrzhor's coat was personal. Each individual plate was etched by the Fyrzhor that owned it with the names of his kinship. Kirkas' fingers traced over the letters of Kösnyrilûmdir. Then, his son. It was unlikely he'd ever see either again...

Boom-doom-boom.

The Fyrdûr shook away the thought, his hauberk of chain rattling beneath the plates. He shifted the fauld just below the plate-coat to align better the thin lames and thicker tassets that fell over each cuisse fastened about his thighs – one could never be too careful with the legs. Indeed, one broken knee, or torn ligament, and a Fyrzhor was prone. Their stature was bad enough, they didn't need to be any closer to the ground than that. The cuisse was bolted to the poleyn over his kneecap, which in turn was bolted to the pair of greaves guarding his shins. The flames that rode up his legs and torso started here, mimicking the rising fire of the Ilaeon, the heart-forge of the Cinderstride. To the enemy, it was as if they were charging through fire, and riding the flames into battle.

As king, Kirkas took one comfort beyond his men, but one comfort only. He had imported a hide of *wuhlf* fur to line his boots. They were a heavy set, with steel capping toe and heel, but their inner lining was leather. When the fur arrived, he personally went to work to fit the luxury in. Unlike many before him, Kirkas was a Fyrdûr of adventure, and, in the wilderness, cold feet would lead to a quick death. Even in their mountains of fire and ash, the nights brought frost and a gripping chill along the peninsula.

Boom-doom-boom.

He moved to the window. It had been three years since he left the tower; in all that time, the Cinderstride was preparing for war. They saw what was to come, and would be ready.

Boom-doom-boom.

He scanned the outskirts. The day had finally arrived.

Boom-doom-boom.
The enemy was in the pass.

Köslûm saw the flood, black as his own skin, wash over the mountains far away, dark and deathly shapes against the setting sun. They poured over the rise and rolled into the valleys to the outer gates of Seerhold. He could imagine it now – his brother on the front lines, leading the defense of the wall, the battalions of Fyrzhor in tri-tiered echelon formations, shoulder to shoulder a step behind the next. If that line broke, and the enemy breached the wall, the soldiers would reform into phalanxes, three by three, in the tower's yard, so as pressed would stay cohesive, formidable units. They would attempt to regroup at the tower's inner gate, but gods forbid if the abominations reached the gate... *May the Ninth's strength be with you, brother,* he prayed, *may your spirit carry forth your eternal flame past Shadow if you fall.*

He focused his attention on the bay. The Cinder Daughters were ushering the *ildaini* into the ships at berth; many reached capacity in room faster than weight. *What of honor? Are we to roam without a home like the Nithûr?* he thought. *Is that to be our fate?* While that terrible pride was his first concern, a second and more pressing fear drew him into a terrifying fatestream. If the Fyrzhor left the

Cinderstride, could their race survive? There was not a single man, woman, or child across Aegis who knew the secrets of the Fyrzhor, the mysteries of their black race, especially this one: The Fyrzhor only bore sons. The Cinder Daughters were not children of Fyrzhor males; they simply existed, and even the Fyrdûr couldn't tell you how they came into being. They would marry and bear the children of the Fyrzhor, but every scion was a son. There had not been a female birth since time began, or so the legends said. And if the Fyrzhor were to leave the Ildûm'tyr behind, while they could take the Cinder Daughters with them, eventually each of those mothers would fall to Shadow, and the race would be left alone, without heirs, and without a way to procreate. Had his brother thought of this? "There has to be another way," Köslûm said aloud, glancing back to Seerhold, casting a great Shadow along the Ildûm'tyr in the dusk. "They say we drink the blood of the gods, brother, that wizardry is woven through our steel and that we can see the future. Those myths were born of legends, legends that bore truth. They came from battles like this that we fought – that we won!" Köslûm slammed his fist against the wall and screamed in anger.

He about-faced and raced down the Beacon Tower's stairwell, "I will not run away."

Kirkas heaved the gre ataxe over his head and cleaved through three nightmares in one mighty swing. The ruins of the gate lay beneath his feet, and the host of abominations swarmed about him. The echelon was in pieces and the phalanxes were failing; there were just too many in the yard. "Fall back!" he cried out to his men. "Into the tower!"

Kirkas caught an enemy's strike between the finger joints of his gauntlet, spiked for hand-to-hand combat, and twisted away. He blew past a dozen more creatures before slipping through the colossal stone ingress of Seerhold's keep. The massive doors were slammed shut behind him, crushing a nightmare between the obsidian slabs. "We hold here!" he called, and motioned his men to form a six by six phalanx at the entrance to the Bellows. It was a small shaft between the foyer and the stairwell to the throne room far above, and it was the only thing that mattered, now. "We need to give Köslûm more time. Nothing gets through that threshold."

Something more powerful than the feral pawns of darkness slammed into the doors. Everyone jumped except for Kirkas; he knew the swarm was one thing, but power was another – they had to have something bigger, and here it was, for this very purpose. He saw the fear in his soldiers' eyes. It was time to be their King. "Hey! What are you afraid of, boys? Those things are uglier than we are!"

The soldiers laughed.

"Loosen yourselves up!" Kirkas shook violently and raised his arms, bellowing.

His soldiers followed suit.

"Not for a thousand years has an enemy breached the Cinderstride! The Fyrzhor do not bend; we do not break. We fight on, and we stand tall!"

On cue, the stone doors crumbled inward, and what looked like a living mountain drove into the tower. It had no weapon, but bore down on the Fyrzhor with fists thrice their size. Kirkas leapt out of the way, and looked past the monstrosity. The abominations followed en masse; the swarm drove toward the phalanx at the shaft, while the mountain took to the stairwell. "Forget the tower, don't let them pass!"

The Fyrzhor did as they were told, and stood fast, a solid wall of immovable steel. The abominations' teeth, claws, and the bloodstained iron taken from their march down the Wreatheland were no match for the armor of the black elves. Regrettably, it didn't matter.

Kirkas flew to the aid of a soldier dragged away from the phalanx, drowning under a furious assault. At least a dozen of the things were atop him. By the time the king severed enough limbs and thrashed enough skulls to force his way through, the soldier's head was no longer attached to his body. *If we survive this,* he thought, *every Fyrzhor here is getting a helmet.*

A flash of light engulfed the stairwell, and moments later, the living mountain tumbled down it, dead into the hall. The Ninth would not fight for them, but he would fight for himself it seemed.

When he readdressed his surroundings, the foyer's floor was littered with bodies. He never thought an enemy could be so ruthless, care so little for their own survival. There was no such thing as a tactical strike or a well-placed thrust, no training or experience; these creatures simply scratched, slashed, and rent through anything they could reach until it was torn to shreds. This would become a battle of attrition, *and for that*, he knew, *we will lose.*

The abominations began ignoring the wall of Fyrzhor by scrambling over them to reach the pitch beyond. He prayed his brother was already gone, that their sons had taken to the sea by now. Köslûm would be a good king until Kirkas' own son was old enough to be anointed. Still, it was not a time for sadness, but for joy and spirit in the heat of battle; he would die as the Shield-King he was, and make certain Köslûm had the time to get away. "Fight on! Fight on!" he called.

"Stand tall! Stand tall!" the cry came back.

Köslûm saw the smoke rising around the tower on the horizon. Seerhold was lost. His brother was dead. He was now the acting Fyrdûr until Kirkas' son, Kirainyranûm, came of age. Grieving was something the Fyrzhor simply didn't do; in fact, the loss of his brother may have been the greatest loss for the Fyrzhor in a century, but it meant he was no longer disobeying orders. He didn't have to leave, and his plan already removed any means to do so.

As bedlam reached the pass leading into the bay's promenade, the Cinder Daughters tied the last knots in his strategy. Every sail had been torn away from its mast and tied together to weave a fence-like barrier along the wharf's perimeter, between the street and the berths. It lay loose as the abominations crashed into the few echelons remaining at Köslûm's disposal. *Each of your names will be remembered when this battle is won*, he swore. As the waves of darkness were stalled, the Cinder Daughters took dozens of jars of pitch and soaked the fence. They spread the rest of the fuel across the street, black oil shimmering in the moonlight. They were ready.

Köslûm motioned the Lûmryn'war; its light shot down to what endured of the Fyrzhor in the pass. They fell back through the overwhelming masses and clamored across the wet street; their heavy boots had no trouble traversing the slippery terrain – they could smell the pitch, and knew what was to come. The taloned, hoofed, or bare metatarsal feet of the nightmares were not so lucky. They were slowed, slipping and tumbling through the liquefied path. As soon as the soldiers leapt over the fence at rest, it was pulled taught by the Cinder Daughters at the end points and secured to poles they drove into the mud. As the first wave of abominations reached the street's center, Köslûm lit the fence.

The fire caught violently in a tidal wave that spat from the hemp to the street, igniting the whole path ablaze. What happened next shot through Köslûm's heart, a lance of dread through his maille and deep into his chest. He'd never been as dumbfounded or afraid as he was in this moment; and the very world felt unnatural to him now. *What has Aegis allowed on her plane?* he thought. The daemons were not stopped by the six-foot wall of flame. The creatures willingly ran into the fire in a vain attempt to reach the Fyrzhor, to see won their sole purpose to exist. And they perished, one after another after another. This saw a dozen or so reach the perimeter; they started hacking away at the sails, but the Cinder Daughters at point responded immediately and cut them down.

The nightmares fell dead in troves, but higher numbers were reaching the barrier every minute, trampling over their fallen predecessors to reach the fence unscathed – there were so many, the bodies were extinguishing the flames. Köslûm couldn't believe his eyes. He tried to see through the flames to the ranks beyond, but all he saw was a rising tide of black over black, abominations over bodies, descending over the hill of their grotesque, untended dead. Before he could determine just how many more filled their ranks, the sail in front of him was sheared in two, and the nightmares poured past. He had failed, and now there was nowhere to go: "Phalanxes! Three by three at the berths!" he cried out to the remaining soldiers. "Daughters, back to back!"

Everyone in earshot obeyed. Everyone out of earshot followed suit as they saw the line fall. Phalanxes three by three were formed at each mooring, and the vicars paired off wherever they could. He'd never seen the Cinder Daughters fight, but this night they exerted a mercilessness unlike any he'd witnessed in his life. They were fighting not just for their lives, but the lives of their sons, the future of the Fyrzhor race and—

The sting cut through his clavicle, forthwith to his spine, and Köslûm dropped. He was on his back, and when he realized this, he knew he'd see his brother soon. The Fyrzhor didn't wear helmets; one of the nightmares saw this and took advantage, driving a spear down through the gap between his pauldrons at the neck. *Why don't we wear helmets, again?* he found himself asking, though surely there were more pressing matters. Staring up at the *evari* shining brilliant through the smoke, he felt his blood spilling down his plate and pooling beneath him. In seconds, Shadow would take him, his eternal flame riding alongside his brother's. Before it did, he heard the cry:

"Fight on! Fight on!"

Kirkas! He'd survived, and was somewhere behind the enemy. That meant the nightmares were not endless, and that everything from that flank on back had been defeated.

"Stand tall! Stand tall!" the cry came from the soldiers, the Cinder Daughters, and the sons aboard the ships at berth. They knew it was their king calling to them; it was their king in all his glory to win the day.

Köslûm knew his seconds were gone. His time had come. Nevertheless, for consciousness he fought. His eyes burned, and tears fell, but he fought. His strength failed him, but his will remained. He struggled to hold his last breath tighter than he'd ever held the love of a Cinder Daughter. He wrestled to retain the air in his lungs longer than he'd ever challenged his brother in the Emberpools. Then, appearing above him in a haze of smoke and vision blurred by Shadow, was Kirkas. The Fyrdûr's eyes were crystal bright in the moonslight, and his hand was cool to the touch. It wrapped around the back of Köslûm's neck, gripped tight, and lifted his brother into his arms. Köslûm knew no words could escape his lips to show his thanks and love for his kin without releasing his final breath. He held it long enough to give Kirkas a trembling nod. Slipping from the light, his eyes drifted, and Köslûm saw his reflection in his brother's crown. In that moment, he knew the truth in the myth, the legends of the Fyrzhor realized. He knew he would be remembered, and he knew his people would survive. With that knowledge, he exhaled.

The Nameless

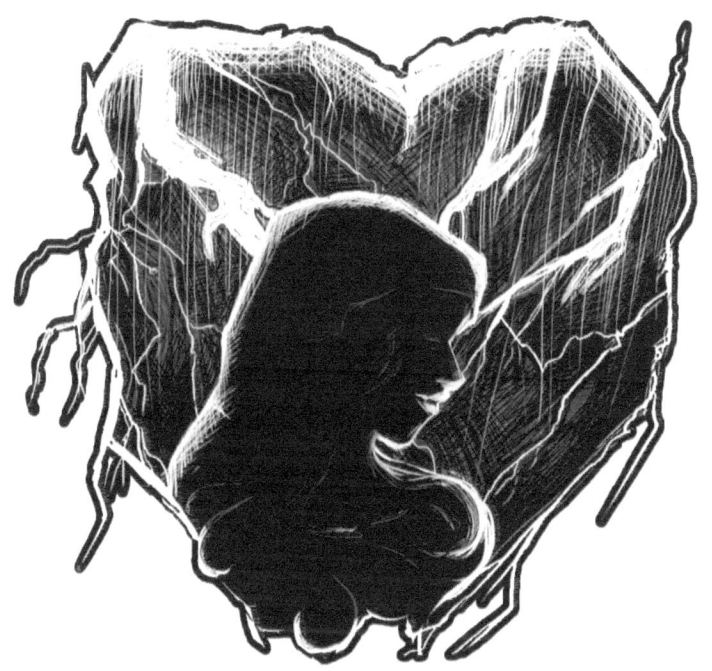

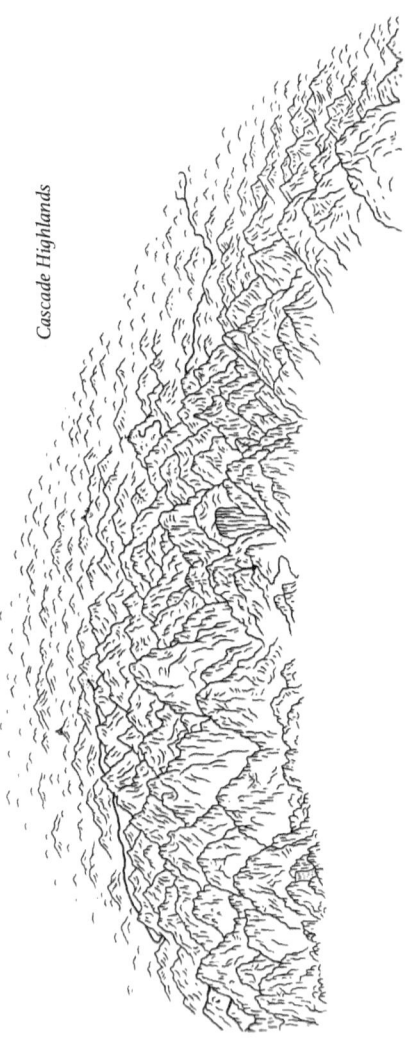

Cascade Highlands

*...being a short story during the Age of Origin,
approximately in the year 972...*

The sword pierced her heart. Her adversary's eyes flashed with grim satisfaction before the emerald glazed over: *How many times had this Bayman killed,* she wondered, *how many deaths were a result of his life?* Her enemy's steel, thrice-folded and Fyrzhor-forged, was as ice against the rush of warm blood escaping her body. Today, over the Cascade Highlands, she was dead. Or soon to be. She wondered if any Nithûr would survive to bury her.

Her enemy's eyes shifted, readying to engage his next victim. Would his prey be a herdsman of the north, a woman *pazhûr* like herself, hooded and wandering? Or was it a nomad's child? Was this the Nithûr's penitence for years of political evasion; did they deserve this for a past of arrogant religious individuality?

No, she refused. In these hills of shepherds and sheep, the soldiers and saints of Chaos could not triumph, would not pass without a fight – the Nithûr were few and far between as it was. When she saw the Bayman's tendons tighten along his wrist, readying to draw the blade from its current sheath – her chest cavity – she snapped both hands to the metal and gripped tighter than a child to its toy.   That was all she humored this physical manifestation of war was, now.   The Bayman's expression, speechless, bewildered, would have brought laughter to her lips if only he would live to forgive her. At heart, the nomadic origins of the Nithûr were peaceful to a fault. She didn't want to kill the man, but she had no choice. Today, her heart was lost. *May the Elzhri absolve me*, she prayed.

The Bayman jerked back with the might of a man who'd spent most of his years going from one war to the next, a battle in the front lines to a brawl in the local pub; however, she held fast to his pointy stick. It dug deep into her calloused hands, but her pain receptors had already shut down from their initial overload at his strike. Unfortunately, she would need that sensation back for the moments to come – the agony might prove unbearable; thus, she closed her eyes and breathed.

The sun was too hot, the air too dry, the day too clear – she needed to concentrate. *Rainfall... The rainfall last night...* She forced the thought to the front of her mind to discharge the heart's distraction of reality. She drew herself into the memory and focused on it – one hand dropped from the blade of steel and fell to the blades of grass softening her current deathbed. There, her fingers caught a drop of dew miraculously clinging to life amidst the carnage of the morning battle. The dewdrop centered her desire, and she knew the ripples she felt through her skin were carried on nature's mystery by Aegis' blessing, something mighty yet finite, soothing yet spellbound. The veil clouding the memory of the night before cleared; she heard the Stormstone winds that speared the valleys, felt the thunder drum deep and booming between the hills, then saw the lightning flash against the *Evar'tûm* across the back of her eyelids – it was in that moment, she opened them.

Her irises sparked. Embers fell from the corners of her eyes and singed the ground beneath her auburn muss. Simultaneously, her fingers ignited and lightning spit from the flesh at their tips; it surged up the enemy's means of murder and punctured the Bayman's heavy plate. She was manipulating the very energy of the world, the spirit of Aegis, to do her bidding. The current punched through his maille, seared past a thick *bain*-hide jerkin layered beneath, bore through the pores of his skin and struck his heart. Its final beat echoed between her own temples only once, before it fell silent.

As her enemy dropped to the ground in a heap and a clamor, she kept her grip on the weapon he finally let go for his journey unto Shadow. Aground flat and controlled, she stared at her new subject of attention – the sword was the tricky part. If she just pulled it out, there could be irreparable damage. Regardless, she was already bleeding out. However, done correctly, there was a long shot for survival. Aegis already blessed her once; *will you help me again?*

She focused on the steel's edge, and allowed it to gouge into her palms so the folds were close to one with her grasp. The molecular structure of its Fyrzhor origin was complicated, as dredgers' wizardry always was when coated into their smithing, so she followed the lay lines in each hammer strike against anvil, pinned down the shatter points and avoided them, then felt the hand of its maker. When the whole of the weapon was sketched out in her mind, its design was hers to control. She induced and compressed time, and wrought the crux of age into its core. A thousand years of decay consumed it, until the blade became brittle.

As sand across stone, it blew away in the breeze and was no more.

Whilst the sword was gone, the wound remained. She drew upon the power of Aegis a third and final time. Exhausted, she dug her freed hand into the wound, and found her heart.

Clutching it gently tight, she felt the beat of her life fading away – and fast. She focused on what it was before the assault, healthy and loving and bright. She fixated on the grass between the fingers of her hand dug back into the earthen cradle, soft and wild and pure. Trusting in faith, a true Nithûr of conviction and hope, she let Aegis do the rest.

In the end, if she was meant to live, she'd live.

A motionless lifetime passed in the knowledge that, at any time, an enemy could find her prone. Instead of panic, she felt at peace. She recalled the start of the war, or at least, when her people found out about it. When the Thrush-King called to the Highlands, they refused to answer, refused to lend aid to the cause in manpower or trade. This War of Shattering, as all the realms called it now, was not their own, but far away. How wrong, they were. Six great battles saw the war end, won by mortals over a mad god, and a retreating flood of Chaos followed. The retreat of darkness fled over the Stormstones and careened down the mountains into the Highlands where it crashed into the Nithûr in all fear and fury. That's where this battle began. Now, because of their infernal hubris, no one from the Wreatheland to the Reignhearth would come to their aid or help them recover. They were seen as cowards by all, and that cowardice was paid for today in the lives of the innocent.

The bleeding stopped. Her heart beat steadily. She slipped her hand back out of the wound no longer open as it was, now a small crack in her cavity. She ripped a piece of her robe at the hem and pulled a strip of unused leather from her belt to tie a patch about her chest. In a cycle's time, there would be nothing left but a scar.

The scar... She needed to stand now, and see the scars of her home.

Not without difficulty, she rose to her feet, and looked over the hills. The sun was setting over the Highlands, and there were more shades of black and red, than there were of brown and green. The cries of the dying and the stain of the dead was almost too much to bear. The enemy had fallen, somehow, someway, defeated; or they passed on and left the remains, but she'd never know. Whosoever won this battle was irrelevant, now. Contrarily, she couldn't help but feel they all lost. The world itself was lost.

She saw five other survivors, silhouettes across the knolls against the blaring sun, and one strange figure to the south. He was neither friend nor foe, standing against the Stormstone's cliff face. His beard fell down the mountainside in a tangle of knots and bounds, like a river of rapids in the fatestreams. The man in tattered grays studied the massacre with intense interest. *Is he staring at me*, she thought, *who is that?*

Who was this? he pondered. With the orange light of the setting sun casting Shadows over the moors, the First knew he'd be no more than a silhouette against the backdrop of the Cascade. This mortal woman intrigued him.

Gripping tight the orb in his pocket that held his eyes in the present, staying the fatestreams from taking his sight to the future, Aeginsyr descended the Stormstones. *Who is she?* She, this false sorceress that Aegis allowed to access her spirit, her very womb, to draw such power. *She should've died. I saw it.*

That night, while the bodies burned in their mass grave, Aeginsyr the First, immortal Elzhri, watched the mortal Nithûr woman weep. He never asked her name, because it didn't matter. For all his interest, she was just one more hero – nameless.

Other works released under Canticles Productions

Canticles Mythos Series
Volume I: The Age of Origin
Volume II: The Age of Shadow (forthcoming, Fall 2020)
Anthology I: The First Sires
Anthology II: The First Fallen
Anthology III: The First Fires (forthcoming, Winter 2020)

Canticles Literature Series
Poet's Compendium I: Hand in Hand
Sybil and the Floot-Snoot (forthcoming, Winter 2018)
Poet's Compendium II: Eye for Eye (forthcoming, Winter 2019)
The Return of the Rings (forthcoming, Spring 2018)

Canticles Albums
Aria I: The Heroes of Our Days
Aria II: The Shadows of Our Past
Aria III: The Nature of Our Love (forthcoming, Winter 2020)
Aria IV: The Parting of Our Ways (forthcoming, Winter 2021)
The Life and Lore of Wintertide (forthcoming, Winter 2019)
Faerû's Lullaby [Single]
The Öleander's Kiss [Single]
The Pursuit of Stars [Single]
To Follow a Broken Heart's Beat [Single]

on PATREON

Canticles' vision took flight in the Summer of 2016,
and is now a Patreon-Based, independent Production
Company.

A little about us:
We're based in the Midwest, not Hollywood.
We offer originality, not rehash and remakes.
We are family-friendly, and have something for everyone!

Join the adventure today!
Be a part of the Canticles Family!
Become a Patron at:
www.patreon.com/canticlesproductions

ISBN 978-0-692-16867-7